Jennifer Rae was raised on a farm in Australia by salt-of-the-earth farming parents. There were two career options for girls like her—become a teacher or a nurse. Rather disappointingly for her dear old dad, she became neither.

All she'd ever wanted to do was write, but she didn't have the confidence to share her stories with the world. So instead she forged a career in marketing and PR—after all, marketing and PR professionals are the greatest storytellers of our time!

But following an early mid-life crisis several years ago Jennifer decided to retrain and become a journalist. She rediscovered the joy of writing and became a freelance writer for some of Australia's leading lifestyle magazines. When she received a commission to interview a couple of romance-writers for a feature article Jennifer met two incredible Australian authors whose compelling stories and beautiful writing touched her cold, cynical heart.

Finally the characters who had been milling around Jennifer's head since her long years on the farm made sense. Jennifer realised romance was the genre she had to write. So, with little more than a guidebook borrowed from the local library and a you-can-do-this attitude, Jennifer sat down to release her characters and write her first romance novel.

When she's not ferrying her three children to their various sports, musical endeavours and birthday parties, you can find Jennifer at the boxing gym, out to dinner with her friends or at home devouring books.

Jennifer has lived in New Orleans, London and Sydney, but now calls country New South Wales home.

Other Modern Tempted™ titles by Jennifer Rae:

SEX, LIES & HER IMPOSSIBLE BOSS
CONFESSIONS OF A BAD BRIDESMAID

**This and other titles by Jennifer Rae are available
in eBook format from www.millsandboon.co.uk**

To my sisters from other misters:
Sonja Screpis, Carla Poole, Tiffany Steel
and Julie Whittington.
Without you I'd understand nothing
and laugh a lot less.
Massive love, my beautiful friends. x

In the darkness of the bar, with the slow, sexy beat of the music in the background, Jack was looking... *delicious.*

He saw her and smiled, and she steeled herself against the anxious flutter in her chest.

Don't look at his smile...look at his teeth. White, straight—perfect. No, not helping. Look away.

His hair. Look up.

It looked thick and wavy and it was being held up over his forehead. Very nice hair.

Don't look at his hair.

His eyes. Dark and velvety. Chocolaty. Sexy. Bedroom eyes.

Definitely don't look there.

A lazy layer of dark stubble sat on his jaw. It made him look a little rougher, a little more manly—maybe even a little dirty.

Brooke swallowed hard and pulled at the collar of her shirt. She'd wanted to look sophisticated, in charge and in control. But now all she felt was exposed. She tried to cover herself up a little before pushing her lips into a wide smile and attempting to saunter towards him.

He smiled and said, 'You look incredibly sexy tonight. Hot date?'

Dear Reader

Something that has always fascinated me is finding out why people make the choices they do and where their emotions stem from. Reality TV is supposed to be a fly-on-the-wall interpretation of real life, but often it's not. It's manipulated to increase drama and sex appeal.

This thought led me on to social media, and the way people use that to manipulate the way people interpret life. Often it's through a filter, and supposedly there are only 'good hair' days. Modern dating has become an exciting but scary place. All it takes is a 'like' on Instagram and a couple of Snapchats and next thing you're tearing each other's clothes off on the floor. *Before* you get to know each other. *Before* you consider the realities of spending time with that person.

We live in an age of filtered reality—and it ain't changing any time soon. But I'm old school. I'd rather meet someone *in person* and find out whether they're a sandwich short of a picnic or if they exude a strange smell, rather than 'like' them on social media and think later.

Brooke and Jack's involvement in a reality TV show skews the way they look at life, love and each other. It takes time spent alone with each other for them to realise that the only way to fall in love—*really* fall in love—is to switch off, push aside pre-judgements and filtered realities and reach deep into each other's souls. Love is *not* a filtered reality. It's dirty and messy, heartbreaking and exhilarating. But when Jack and Brooke realise they need to experience it to feel it their lives can really begin.

Jennifer Rae x

www.jenniferraeromance.com

WHO'S CALLING THE SHOTS?

BY
JENNIFER RAE

First published in Great Britain 2015
by Mills & Boon, an imprint of Harlequin (UK) Limited,
Eton House, 18-24 Paradise Road, Richmond, Surrey, TW9 1SR

© 2015 Jennifer Rae

ISBN: 978-0-263-25723-6

Harlequ
renewa
sustain:
to the l

Printed
by CPI

1

form

CHAPTER ONE

TWELVE PAIRS OF long eyelashes blinked at Jack Douglas. Some of the women were smiling, and some looked as if they were about to burst into a blubbering mess of tears. It was time.

'Congratulations, ladies. You've all made it.'

Squeals, screams and loud relieved sighs followed his announcement.

This day had started like the previous seven. A hundred women at his door, all wanting the same thing. A chance to meet their *Perfect Match*.

'Excuse me.'

The squeals were subsiding and being replaced by excited chatter. Jack watched as the women—virtual strangers this morning—hugged each other. How did women *do* that? Go from open disdain to long-lost best friends in hours? He had known people for years without knowing their last name, let alone throwing his arms around them.

One of the lip-chewing women was in front of him, not hugging anyone. She was standing too close. He looked down. She was a petite woman—tiny, actually. So small he could possibly pick her up and carry her under one arm. Pretty. With a hopeful look in her big green eyes. He swallowed and gave himself a mental uppercut. *Not your problem.*

'Yes?'

He waited for it—the feeling of her tiny little arms around him. He took a step back. She stepped closer. Not only was she going to touch him without permission, she was a close talker. He folded his arms and lifted his chin. Message couldn't be clearer.

'I think there's been a mistake. I shouldn't be here. I should be in one of the other rooms, with the losers.'

She batted her long eyelashes and pulled her lips back into a thin line. She had a wide mouth with full lips, so it looked strange all puckered like that. Jack let his forehead furrow.

'There's no mistake. You've been chosen as a contestant. You're one of the lucky ones.' He smiled, hoping that would satisfy her and she'd step away.

She smiled and a deep dimple formed in her cheek.

'The thing is, I only came here for my sister. She was the one who wanted to get on the show. I'm only here for…support. You should probably check your list. Her name is Madeline Wright—not Brooke Wright.'

Her hands waved as she spoke, and because she was so close the hand holding her phone hit him on the arm. He flinched, but refrained from letting it show on his face.

'The names are correct. Everyone in this room is a winner.'

'But I don't want to *be* here!'

Jack's eyebrows shot up at her fierce announcement. She didn't want to be here? Jack let his eyes run the length of her body. She was dressed in a crisp white shirt and a black skirt to her knees. Clearly she was trying to look professional, but her slightly messy hair and killer body made her look anything but. She looked sexy. Tanned and athletic. As if she didn't belong in those constricting clothes but outside in the sunshine.

Which was where he'd rather be right now. But he was here, trying to get this show off the ground. He wished he was more excited about it. He needed to be—this show was his ticket out—but something was niggling at him. Something he couldn't put his finger on.

It wasn't the format: twelve women competing in a number of challenges in order to win the chance to go on a date with one of the twelve men who had been chosen to match them perfectly. The more challenges they won the more dates they went on. By the end the audience would find out if the man chosen to be their match was the man who had been pegged as their *Perfect Match*. It was fun and interesting and fairly straightforward.

And it wasn't the contestants that bothered him. He'd hand-chosen them all. Even this one. The woman who didn't want to be here. He remembered her audition tape. She'd seemed funny and smart, and he remembered her eyes. A strange dark green. He remembered choosing her. Her eyes had attracted him, but it was her smile that he remembered. A smile that was definitely not present on her face now.

'Did you sign the contract that all the ladies signed before being interviewed by our producers?'

'Well…yes.' The dimple disappeared and colour slashed across her cheeks. 'But…'

'Then you're on the show. We start filming the day after tomorrow.'

Jack pushed a foot back. She was too close and he didn't like close. But she was quick. She reached out and grabbed at his forearm. He stilled. His whole body stiffened. She was touching him and it felt intimate. Wrong. Too personal. His body remained still as the warmth from her fingers spread across his forearm and up past his elbow. Warm and soft, with a firm grip. The back of his neck prickled with heat.

'No,' she said, those eyes of hers narrowing. 'There's been a mistake. I can't go on the show. I'm only here as a reserve. I would be hopeless. I'm not even looking for a husband. I'm marriage-averse. Like, *really* averse. I'd rather chew my own arm off than walk down the aisle.'

Jack tried to move, but her arm was still on his arm and it was all he could think about. He forced his mind into gear. Slowly, carefully, he reached over and gripped her hand. It was as small as the rest of her. Dainty. Slight. But her grip was firm. He prised her fingers clear of his arm and relief swam across his shoulders immediately.

Her eyes opened wide. She was clearly not appreciating being manhandled. But he pushed her hand away and stepped back. Her big green eyes stared at him. Her head cocked to one side and something in her gaze changed. First to confusion, then something else. Something more smug.

'Is my hand bothering you?'

'No.' He smiled. *Charm.* Time to turn on the charm. It always worked. 'As much as I appreciate a beautiful woman touching me, I'm afraid I'm going to have to leave you for your perfect match. After all—that's what you're here for. *Perfect Match*—the only show on TV where we make sure the man you marry is the man of your dreams!'

His marketing team would be proud of that speech.

Jack pulled his face into a wide grin flashing the set of teeth his father had paid thousands of dollars to fix. And reminded him about frequently.

Her hands folded tightly across her chest. 'Look... Jack, is it?'

He nodded tightly. They were definitely not on a first-name basis, but he had to keep the peace here. Nothing could go wrong this time.

'Jack…' Her smile changed. Dimples formed in her cheeks and she fluttered her eyelashes.

She was good. But she wasn't that good. She was trying to use her looks and her charm to get her own way—that much was obvious. Little did this twittering sparrow know that he'd written the book on that game.

'I understand that it's probably a pain to change things now, but I have to tell you I really can't do this. I'm not great around cameras and I'm quite shy—and to be honest there's not really much interesting about me. I'm dull. I'll send your viewers to sleep. Wouldn't it be better to give the spot to someone more exciting? My sister Maddy ticks all those boxes. Seriously—you really should reconsider.'

Jack blinked. Her speech had been a passionate one. His mind wandered back to that audition tape. She'd made fun of herself, pulled faces, clearly not taking it too seriously. She'd smiled that amazing smile a lot on the tape, but she wasn't smiling today.

Mick had said no to her straight up—said she'd be trouble. But there had been something about her…something that had caught his eye. Something that had made him keep watching. She said the viewers wouldn't want to watch her, that she was dull, but he couldn't disagree more. Those eyes, that smile…that body. She'd make perfect viewing. Especially now he knew she didn't want to be here. People out of their comfort zone always made excellent reality TV.

'Our decisions have been made and I don't think you give yourself enough credit. You don't seem dull at all. A little pushy—but definitely not dull.'

Her brows furrowed. 'Pushy? I'm not *pushy*. I'm just telling you the facts.'

'Then let me tell you some facts. You're on the show. You signed a contract. We'll see you back here at nine a.m. the day after tomorrow.'

She didn't say anything, but he watched her chest rise and fall as she breathed deeply.

'I don't think you understand—I can't go on this show.'

'Then perhaps you should have thought of that before you applied.' Her eyes were big and her shoulders slumped. He felt himself falter. *No*. He couldn't do that again. He couldn't feel sorry for her. This was her problem—not his. His job was to make this show a success—not to get her out of the hole she'd dug for herself.

'Think of this as an opportunity. What do you need? Publicity? Money? Hell—you may even meet your perfect match. What woman doesn't want that?'

As soon as he'd said it he knew it had been the wrong thing to say. Her cheeks pinked. Her mouth opened, then closed. Her arms unfolded and she stood with feet shoulder-width apart, fists clenched.

'That's not what I'm here for,' she said tightly, clearly trying to stay controlled. 'I don't want to be here. My sister can take my place; she's the one who wants to be here. She's the one who's looking for love. She's wanted to marry since she was five years old. Trust me, you don't want me. Like I said before—I would *not* make very good viewing.'

'You're making good viewing right now, beautiful.'

Jack let his eyes sweep over her. A compliment always calmed the savage beast. Compliments rolled off his tongue easily, but this time there was a bit of truth in his hollow words. She was a beautiful woman. A nice heart-shaped face, and those perfectly placed big green eyes. She looked healthy, tanned and fun, and she was making his body stand still and take notice. Their male audience would love her.

He shifted his feet. Something grabbed at him. A strange, quiet pull inside him that he recognised immediately but pushed aside. No. He couldn't feel anything. Not for her or anyone else. He couldn't think of any of these women as different from each other. They were all the same. And none of them was anything to him—nor would they ever be. Especially not her.

The way she looked up at him was starting to make something else shift. She stepped forward until her breasts were almost touching his still folded arms. Heat radiated from her but he didn't step back. The scent of her perfume touched his nose and kept him still. Something rumbled inside him. He pushed it down. *No.* Not his problem. Not his anything.

'I'm not here for your viewing pleasure. I'm not here for *anyone's* viewing pleasure. And I'm not going on your stupid show.'

Jack felt his smile falter; she was getting serious now and it was time he did too. She needed to know the rules of this game, and she needed to play by those rules.

'Let me tell you a little about the TV business, darlin'.'

She flinched when he called her *darlin'*, just as he'd thought she would. She didn't like to be patronised—that much was clear. Smart woman. Smart women were much harder to deal with, but he'd done it before. He could deal with her.

'When you sign a contract, your soul belongs to me.' That was a lesson he'd learned years ago. When he'd first sold his own soul.

'I beg your pardon?'

Her voice changed. It became clipped, professional. The voice of a woman who could turn herself into someone else quickly. She straightened her spine and ran a hand over her hair, smoothing it as if trying to take the mess out of it and make it look neater and more business-like. It didn't work. She still looked young and fun and as if she belonged on a beach somewhere in a skimpy bikini.

Jack's producer's mind kicked in. The beach. Perfect for the first episode. And no wetsuits—he'd make the girls dress in bikinis—what a first great ep. He'd open with a faux *Baywatch* running sequence. The girls running along the beach…chasing the men! Gold! It would rate its butt off.

Her voice brought him back to the moment. It was tight and high and way too loud.

'My soul does not—nor will it ever—belong to you. I signed a contract, yes. But now I choose to break that contract. What do I need to do? Pay you some money? Fine. But don't assume that you own me—or that I won't fight you to get what I want.'

Jack's cheeks heated. Her fire was surprisingly sexy. She'd gone from twittering sparrow to swooping eagle in seconds, but those green eyes remained the same. Strong, wide, green as an open ocean and beautiful.

Jack shook it off. He couldn't think of her as beautiful. He couldn't think about her at all. That was when things got complicated and he got into trouble. This woman was definitely one who could cause trouble. Too smart. Too pretty. And she knew what she was worth, which made her dangerous. He didn't need dangerous. He needed this show to be a hit.

Maybe Mick was right and she would be too much trouble. But, then again, that was exactly what the show needed. She was perfect. Bad-tempered, unwilling and impossible to control. That was what this show was lacking. He knew she was a risk, but he needed to take some risks. If he didn't he'd continue to be the man who'd got his job through nepotism rather than because he deserved it. He should leave. Get a job as a garbage man. Far away from his father and far away from all the talk of him not deserving his job. But the truth was this station—and by extension his father—owned him. Until he proved he could finally produce a hit show he was stuck. And so was she. And as long as he didn't get sucked in to her sob story he was out of danger.

She stepped forward and he stepped back—away from her—but she managed to step forward again.

'Don't you run away from me. I need this sorted. I cannot stay.'

Jack felt the air thicken and his breath shorten. Her eyes sparked and he felt it deep in his core. Her pretty eyes were ready for a fight. She might be small, but this one didn't need his protection. She was doing a good job of protecting herself.

He let out a breath and sucked in another big one. He could read the way she felt on her face. *Trapped*. He knew the feeling well. But, like him, she would have to figure it out for herself. Like him, she was on her own. A strange feeling of solidarity with this woman crept over him. Two independent souls. Two people who could take care of themselves. Two people who came up swinging no matter how many times they were knocked down.

'I'm afraid you have no choice, Ms Wright. You are now a lucky contestant on *Perfect Match*!'

'Are you kidding me? This is *great* news!'

Brooke stared at her boss, who was also her sister. Her mad sister. Who had convinced her to join in with this ridiculous, absurd scheme. A scheme that was so bonkers Brooke wondered if she'd actually lost all sense of reality for a moment.

'Brooky—it's perfect. I wanted to go on the show because I'm sick of meeting losers. I wanted to meet Mr Right—someone who's been interviewed and vetted so I didn't have to do all the hard work. Which, when you think about it, is a silly reason to go on the show. Interviewing and vetting men is the fun part! But you—you're not there to find love. You're there with your head screwed on—which makes you an even better candidate than me.'

'Maddy—I really don't think it's a great idea...'

Caution shot through Brooke. Maddy always made sense. She was the eldest of the Wright clan, and the most sensible sister. Brooke looked to Maddy whenever she needed advice. But right now Maddy was acting more like Melody, the youngest and loopiest sister.

This scheme to gain promotion for their business was mad. It had been mad when Maddy had thought it up a month ago. It had been mad when Maddy had suggested she come along as 'back-up', and it was even madder now that Brooke was going to have to make a fool of herself in front of the entire country just to sell some gym gear.

'It makes perfect sense, Brooky! I would have been too emotional. I would have been distracted. But you will be perfect! Sensible, straightforward, practical Brooky.' Maddy's animated face softened and she came out from behind her desk to put her arms out. 'Think about it. How much would we have to pay to advertise on prime time TV every night for three months?'

Brooke didn't care about the free advertising this show would expose their gym gear to. She couldn't think about marketing opportunities and how well-known their brand might be if she managed to get their products on the screen. All she could think of was the potential humiliation. When all those millions of people watching realised how bad she was at relationships and love and flirting and all the other rubbish that was sure to happen on this ridiculous show.

Brooke breathed in, then out. That familiar feeling crept over her. She knew what it was and she breathed through it, just as Maddy had taught her all those years ago. She wasn't going to get angry. She was going to explain herself rationally and clearly. Brooke released the fist her hand had formed. Her palm hurt where her fingernails had dug in.

'Thousands, Brooky!'

Maddy threw her arms around her sister and hugged her hard. The hug helped. Brooke felt her sister's love as she let go and held on to Brooke's shoulders.

'You know that because we checked. And we checked because the brand needs help, Brooke. *Major* help. Think about how many people will be watching you. Think about all those lonely, desperate women out there, watching you night after night as a handsome man falls in love with you. They'll be listening to every word you say— and looking at everything you wear. *Everything.* Including your clothes. They'll want to be like you, work out like you, dress like you so they can find the man of their dreams too.'

Maddy was doing what she always did to calm Brooke down. Giving her rational arguments. Explaining things. Talking to her until Brooke started to breathe normally again.

'Maddy…' Brooke started, her voice normal again. 'You're crazy. That's an awfully long shot.'

'It's perfect PR—you even said it yourself at the marketing pow-wow last month. You don't have to tell anyone to buy our products—you just show them how fabulous they look and how well they work and be your amazing self and they will sell themselves.'

Maddy was really working overtime. Brooke could tell she was passionate about this, and she could also tell her sister was working hard to get her excited. But Brooke wasn't buying it.

'Maddy! Listen to yourself. This is ridiculous!'

'No, it's not.' Maddy said, her voice calm, strong and matter-of-fact. 'It's genius. *I'm* a genius. Wright Sports is poised for world domination, little sister.'

'You're not a genius—you're a madwoman. First of all, if you want someone to model the clothes to make women aspire to be like them, you should have chosen Melissa. She's the long-legged, big-boobed beauty in the family. Or even Melody—she's cute and perky and blonde and fun! I'm short and I have a forgettable face and my mouth is too wide.'

Maddy attempted to interject but Brooke held up a hand.

'I don't need you to compliment me, Maddy, which I know you were going to do. I'm just stating facts here. And reason number two why this plan is absolutely bonkers: women will only aspire to be like me if I successfully seduce a man. Which I won't. I can't flirt, I'm awkward and boring, and I am *really* bad at competing. I'm the only one in this family who hasn't won a gold medal in something. And even if I don't fail every challenge I'm sure my appointed "perfect match" will probably kill me in my sleep. You've got the wrong girl, Maddy. Me being me will do more damage to the brand than good.'

'Why do you do that, Brooky?' Maddy asked gently.

Brook bristled. 'I'm not doing anything besides telling you what a terrible idea this is.'

'Brooke, you're beautiful and talented and fabulous. You'll win every challenge and your perfect match will fall for you—just like the entire country will when they see you on the telly. You're exactly the right girl. I *knew* you'd get it—why do you think I made you come along with me?'

'Maddy, I don't need any of your motivational nonsense right now.'

'It's not motivational nonsense. As a matter of fact…' Maddy moved away to go back behind her desk. She drew herself up to her full five foot nine and stared straight at her little sister. 'I think this will be good for you. You need to put yourself out there. It's time you got yourself a man.'

Brooke rolled her eyes. This wasn't the first time she'd heard this lecture. Her four sisters were always telling her she needed to go out more, be more social—meet new people. But the truth was she liked being alone. It was safer that way. She liked her quiet nights in and she didn't need a man bothering her with his opinions and demands…and his lies and broken promises.

'I don't want a man, Maddy.'

'Brooke. It's time you got over Mitch. It's been twelve months.'

Brooke felt the familiar burn of tears in the backs of her eyes. *Mitch.* Even the sound of his name felt like sandpaper rubbing on foam.

'I'm over him, Maddy.' She heard her voice go quiet. She wished it hadn't. She didn't want her sisters to worry about her. She was over Mitch. Of course she was. Why wouldn't she be? Like Maddy said—it had been twelve months.

Something caught in Brooke's throat. Twelve months since she'd decided not to put up with another one of his lies. Twelve months of thinking about all the things she'd say to him if she ever saw him. Something hurt in Brooke's chest. She wasn't in love with Mitch any more, but the anger about what he'd done was still there. She'd tried everything—yoga, meditation, drinking some disgusting concoction Melody called 'calm juice'—but the feeling was still there. A hard ball of anger she couldn't seem to shake.

'It's clear you're not, Brooke. You don't go out; you don't want to meet anyone new. You just sit at home listening to sad music or working out like a demon. Honestly, babe, we're worried about you. You need this. More than me. More than the brand. You need to do something to break you out of this rut.'

Brooke breathed out heavily. She *was* in a rut. It was true. But she was happy in her rut. Happy to push herself to her limits at the family-owned gym and happy to work herself ragged as marketing manager for her family's company.

She excelled at her job. It was the only time she'd ever been close to competing with her sisters. Micky, the second oldest, was the country's leading female equestrian at only twenty, Melody was in line to join their sister Melissa at the next Commonwealth Games, while Maddy, the most successful of all, was a former gold medallist.

Brooke had just achieved her personal best number of pull-ups in a row at the gym. Five. Pathetic. At only four foot nine, and barely fifty-two kilograms, Brooke was smaller, weaker and so much less remarkable than her sisters. But she was very good at data and statistics and predicting trends.

Since leaving school six years ago she'd managed to

help Maddy take their company from a fledgling gym and activewear business to an award-winning national brand, with seventeen retail stores across the country and a dozen new lines ranging from home workout gear to protein powders. But times were tough. Money was tight. And to move to the next level—which they'd all decided it was time for—they needed to up their game.

Publicity. Recognition. That was what they needed. Brooke knew it. But they'd planned for *Maddy* to get on to this stupid TV programme—Brooke had gone there for moral support and some sort of pathetic back-up on the off-chance Maddy didn't get it. Brooke hadn't doubted for a second that Maddy would get in. Maddy always won everything... Except this time.

And now, in some cruel, unexpected twist of fate, Brooke was expected to expose herself on a reality show based on the ridiculous premise that there was a *Perfect Match* out there for everyone. But Brooke knew what she had to do. She had no choice. This was her family's future and it was in her hands. Every team she'd ever been on had dumped her, due to her pathetic athletic ability, but her sisters never had. They'd always been there for her. From that first day.

'OK, I'll do it.'

Maddy came around the desk to throw herself at Brooke, but Brooke held her back with an arm.

'I'm going to hate every second, I'm going to regret this with every atom in my tiny body, but I'll do it. For you. And Micky and M'Liss and Melody.'

Maddy smiled her brilliant white smile and pulled her in for a giant hug. 'You might be surprised, little sister—you might end up loving every minute.'

Brooke pulled her face into a massive frown as she was squashed into Maddy's chest, knowing deep, deep down that there was no way in hell she was going to enjoy *any* minute of this humiliating and utterly absurd experience.

CHAPTER TWO

JACK SCHOOLED HIS features into something more gentlemanly. His father's face beamed at him from the big screen TV.

'He's a quality unit, Jack. He can make a hit out of anything. I want you to do anything you can to help him out.'

The hairs on the back of Jack's neck stood erect. It was happening again. Just like last time. Just like every damn time. And, just like last time, he wanted to hit someone. Preferably his father. But since his father was on the screen, not there in person, he'd do more damage to himself and probably have to fork out for a new TV. Not smart.

'I've got it sorted, Max. I don't need any help.' He kept his tone low and calm.

'Now, don't go getting your knickers in a knot, Jacko. Rob Gunn is not there to take over. He's a hit-maker—you should be relieved he's coming on board.'

His father never kept his voice low and calm. When Jack was younger, he'd thought of his father as some kind of god-like Santa Claus. He was big and loud and jolly, and he would fly back home laden with gifts for his only child. He hadn't seen him often, so when he had Jack would hang on every word and lap up any attention he could get. But Jack wasn't a child any more, and he could see his father for what he was. And he no longer believed in Santa Claus.

'Mick and I have this under control. Anyone else joining would just make it messy…'

Jack's father held up a big, beefy sun-reddened hand. 'Like you and Mick had it "under control" last time? We can't afford another stuff-up like that, Jack. I've told you—'

Jack knew his father hated being interrupted. It was one of the few things they had in common. Which was why Jack did it. That, and the fact that his father was moving into uncomfortable territory.

'Max, I told *you* it's under control. I don't need your hotshot. What happened last time won't happen again. Trust me.'

Jack watched as his father's face turned redder, which made his grey hair burn even brighter. Not for the first time during this conversation Jack noticed how old his father was looking. His normally round cheeks were drooping, his fleshy nose was covered in purple veins and his hair looked even thinner and greyer than normal. Jack felt an unusual flash of sympathy for the man. Something he hadn't felt in a long time. Not since he'd grown up and realised that this loud, full-of-life man was an overbearing bully. Jack shook it off. If his father had taught him anything it was to eradicate any emotions when you were talking business.

'You listen to me, boy. I've lined this bloke up to help you. It's all about *you*. Like everything I do—trying to keep your head above water. Trying to keep you afloat. Do you have any idea how much your last little mistake cost our company?'

Jack knew exactly how much it had cost. He'd been

at every meeting. He'd gone through every figure with the accountants and he'd earned back every penny. But there was no use telling his father that. From the look on his face Jack knew the steam train had already left the station. The old man was about to blow and Jack was going to cop it—big-time.

'I started from nothing to build this company, boy. *Nothing*. You have no idea of the things I did to make this company what it is today. And I did it for you. So you would be left with something rather than nothing— like I was.'

Jack leaned back in his chair. He was going to be there a long time. He'd heard this story so many times he could predict what his father was going to say next.

'And what have you done to repay me? Drugs. Women. Wild parties. Deadbeat mates. You haven't appreciated *anything*. I gave you the best of everything—the greatest opportunities. Any kid would gnaw off their right arm to be handed the position of Executive Producer for all our media, the way you were, and what have you done to repay me?'

Jack mouthed the words along with him, knowing full well his father was too blind with his own indignation to notice.

'You've produced a string of reality shows that have ended in fights and lawsuits and disaster. I can tell you now, boy, that's *not* going to happen again. Not on my watch. This time you'd better get it right or you can kiss your inheritance goodbye.'

Jack sighed. 'Like I've said to you a thousand times, Dad—I don't want your money. I don't need your money.'

His father's heavy breaths could be heard through the speakers. Jack saw him knock against the computer he was speaking into, losing his balance a little. Max's lips pursed and released, then pursed and released again. He was thinking. Jack could practically see the old man's mind ticking behind his eyes.

'Maybe not, Jacko. Maybe you would be able to make a few measly bucks on your own. But how 'bout your mother? What would happen to *her*, Jack, if I were to shut up shop, take my money and run?'

And there was the stinger. It pierced Jack's gut and lodged there. Jack's father only had one weapon left to use against Jack. His mother. Who was still in love with his father, for some reason Jack couldn't understand. His mother—who would be devastated if she found out how much Max *didn't* care for her any more.

Jack knew exactly what his father meant. At the moment everything Max had—everything he knew about, anyway—was fifty per cent owned by Jack's mother. But when Jack had discovered his father was having an affair fifteen years ago and threatened to tell his mother Max had told him he'd leave his mother with nothing if he did. He'd made Jack realise how powerless he was and then produced a contract saying he had to stay with the media arm of his father's company until he earned enough money to buy his way out of it.

At nineteen, he'd thought it would be easy. But after station cutbacks, a fall in the economy and a cultural shift towards reality TV, Jack had barely covered costs each year. *Perfect Match* was his chance. It had trialled well in market research and the time was right. Dating shows were rating through the roof, and he'd already had a few bites to syndicate it in the US, the UK and India. This show was his ticket out of here—away from his father and the hold he had over him. But until then his father owned him, and he knew it.

'What's that, Jack? Your smart mouth can't come up with anything intelligent to say?'

Jack's blood sizzled but he held his face steady. He was getting too old for this. He needed to take control—one way or another. He needed to get his father out of his life, and today was going to be the start.

'I'm running this company. I'm in charge. Not you. Goodbye, Max.'

Jack pressed the button that would end the video call. His father's face disappeared. This show would be a hit. And when it was he'd pay his father his money and he'd never look back. And when he'd made his own money his mother wouldn't need his father either. They could both escape from his cage.

'Mick, I need you in here, my friend.' Jack spoke into his phone, his voice back to its low, calm tone.

Mick didn't need to know about that conversation. The crew were jumpy enough as it was, with all the rumours flying around about Max pulling their funding. He didn't need them thinking there would be any changes in management. He needed to keep this ship sailing steady.

'How'd it go with Max, boss?' Mick was a man of few words, but he had an eye for entertainment and was one of the best editors in the business. For a man of such little drama, he knew how to produce one.

'Excellent. Couldn't have gone better,' Jack lied. 'But I've been thinking about the format for the show. I know we were going to introduce the men later in the show, once the girls have had a chance to get to know each other, but I think we should move it forward.'

Mick remained silent.

'Bring the men in and have them decide what challenges they want the girls to do. Have them call the shots so they can decide which girls they want to take on dates.

And I think we should cut it back to only four men. That way the girls will have to fight for a chance to meet their perfect match.'

Mick looked thoughtful. He stood still, moving only his head to stare out of the window behind Jack. Jack was used to him by now. He knew what he was doing. Thinking. He gave him a few minutes.

'Female audience are not gonna like it,' Mick finally said in his quiet voice.

'Exactly. They'll hate it. They'll rage and be indignant and it'll be all over social media. It's a genius idea.'

Jack knew the female audience would hate it. He wasn't even sure if it was a great idea. But he needed this show to be a hit. He needed it to work and work quickly—he couldn't afford for anything to happen like last time. This time he was going to be brutal. He was going to call the shots. He was going to create a drama-filled show that had people tuning in every week. This show was about ratings—not about the people on the show. He had to remember that.

Slowly Mick faced Jack and a stern furrow formed on his weathered forehead. 'They'll kill you.'

They would. They'd slam him in the media. They'd call him a misogynist pig. He wondered how the contestants would react to the change. It was within his rights to change the format. He'd written it into the contract. Reality TV was like that—it needed to be fluid and reactive.

And the girls might not understand—they might have questions. He'd go and see them after this. He was sure he'd be able to win them over—he'd deliberately chosen women he could mould and shape. Except *that* one. Ms Wright. She hadn't seemed very malleable. Gorgeous. Great mouth. Insane body. But not malleable. No, if anyone was going to jack up about this new twist it would be her.

'That little firecracker won't like it,' Jack admitted.

Mick grunted. 'I told you not to put her on the show. I knew she'd be trouble.'

Brooke Wright was the only contestant Mick had objected to. He'd said she'd be trouble, would cause problems and make their job harder. And he had been right. She'd protested from the beginning—not wanting to be on the show, then grumbling when he'd informed them they wouldn't have any contact with their friends and families during the entire six weeks of taping. But she was nothing he couldn't handle. He had learned how to charm women years ago. His father had been his mentor.

'Tell 'em what they want to hear,' his father would say. 'Then do whatever the hell you want anyway!'

He'd always laugh after that. Jack never had. Not when it came to his mother. But after a few awkward 'falling in love with a girl who didn't love him' moments back in high school he'd started to use his father's tactics. And it had worked. Since then he'd been able to get women to do what he wanted—mostly.

Ms Wright, however, might prove to be a bit of a challenge. She tended to get into his personal space. She was a little too confrontational. To be honest, she made him a little uncomfortable. But she wasn't there for him. She was there for the show—to make it a hit. Maybe this would be perfect. This new twist would send her into a new flutter and he'd catch it all on camera. It would be just what he needed.

He pushed down the small flutter of guilt that settled in his chest. He needed to work out the details and amend their choice of men. But first he had to supervise the taping of the first challenge. This time he was going to be there for everything. All the on-camera highlights as well as the off-camera drama. This time he wasn't missing a thing—because this time was his last.

'Tell Gaz to bring the car around, Mick—we're going to see the ladies.'

She could do this. She knew she could do this. It was like lifting heavy weights. Ninety per cent mental, ten per cent physical. All she had to do was believe she could paddle out past the crashing waves, stand up on a thin piece of timber and balance while avoiding sharks and the tumble of the constantly moving water, all the while making sure she kept a smile on her face and her bikini top up—because at least eight cameras were set up on the beach and on jet skis to capture every fall, every failure and every embarrassing facial expression.

Yep, she could do this. For sure. Absolutely. Brooke hitched up the strap of her candy-red Wright Sports bikini and pushed a large ball of nervous energy back down her throat.

She'd never been surfing. It seemed like just another sport to fail at, and her balance wasn't great even on solid ground, so she'd never been tempted to try. But now she had to go out there. Because her crazy sisters thought her coming on this show was their most cunning scheme ever.

'It'll be so good for you, Brooky.'

'It'll help you come out of your shell.'

'People will love you.'

'Imagine what it will do for the brand!'

And the last and most irritating comment of all: 'You might meet your Mr Right.'

She wasn't interested in meeting Mr Right. Or Mr Wrong. She was interested in meeting this month's sales targets. And besides, if Mr Right were out there she was pretty sure he wouldn't be on a surfboard. She had always been more into quiet, sensitive, musician-types. They *got* her. Those carefree athletic types were way too into themselves even to attempt to get her.

'OK, ladies. On your boards.'

The tall, broad-shouldered instructor was hurling instructions at the twelve women lined up on the beach. At least *he* got to wear a wetsuit. Brooke pulled the skimpy fabric to cover up more of her breasts. She'd already argued with the producer over this. Why were they lined up like sheep at a sale yard? Why couldn't they wear wetsuits? Wright Sports made an amazing one, lined with the highest quality Neoprene.

But the producer, Jack Douglas, had done what he always did. Smiled. Turned on his deep, calm voice. His 'you're crazy and I need to calm you down' voice. Stepped back, away from her, and brushed her off.

She was sure she'd got a little red-faced when she'd argued with him about it, but he'd ignored her concerns. Told her that viewers wanted the full beach scene. And then he'd had the hide to tell her she had an amazing body and she should be proud to show it off. Which was totally not the point.

But arguing had been useless. Before too much longer he'd pulled out the old 'you're under contract, sweetheart' card and walked away. So she'd lost. Again. And now she was lined up like a horse in the ring at the Melbourne Cup, awkwardly turning away every time she noticed a camera swivelling towards her butt cheeks.

Most of the other girls didn't seem to care a fig. They were on their boards, laughing, joking—jumping up and down so their bountiful breasts bounced in the sunlight. Brooke's breasts didn't bounce—they were way too small for that—but she did try to smile. For her sisters. For the brand. For her family's business. For the most important people in her life.

That was why she was here, she reminded herself as she heaved the huge board up under her arm and wrapped her fingers tightly around the edge.

Brooke grimaced to the girl on her left—Katy, she remembered. Katy the Lawyer, with her long shiny dark hair and big soulful eyes.

'Let's hope the lifeguards are on duty,' she quipped.

Katy smiled back. 'Hopefully they'll be cute, because I'm sure I'll end up face-down in the sand.'

Brooke felt her shoulders relax. At least most of the other girls were friendly. Something about having to go through this all together had bonded them. That and the fact that the annoying producer had forced them to all live together in a Manly penthouse. As if they were a bevy of pets from the seventies and he was hoping for a little girl-on-girl action.

Brooke felt the steam rise again. At the fact that she was being filmed in a bikini on the beach, doing something she knew she was going to fail at. At the idea of being forced to compete with other women for the chance to go on a date with a man she hadn't even met yet and was sure she wouldn't like anyway. But mostly she fumed at the producer. Jack Douglas.

She knew all about Jack Douglas. After their first disastrous meeting she'd looked him up. The man had only got where he was because of his dear old dad. Although, to be honest, she was in *her* job because of her family, too. But that was different. Jack Douglas was, by all accounts, a womaniser, a publicity whore, a charming pig. And from what she'd seen all of that was true.

Because—seriously—what type of man encouraged this type of sexist, voyeuristic television?

But what annoyed her the most about Jack Douglas was that every time she looked at him she moved. Inside. Deep down. Where she didn't want to move. Especially not for him. But his jaw was so square and his eyes were so dark, and when he crossed his arms he stood tall and strong and so incredibly sexy…it moved her. And she couldn't control it. And that annoyed her. She was so good at controlling herself. She'd taught herself how to control her temper a long time ago. She was now quiet and easygoing and Zen. But Jack Douglas was doing his best to upset her Zen.

'Ladies! Looking beautiful, as always.'

And there he was. Tall, athletic, self-centred, small-minded. The exact opposite of her type. Brooke hadn't had a drink all day, but right then she felt drunk. Drunk on her own indignation. Drunk on humiliation and drunk on the idea that there was no way she was getting out of this mess now she was in it.

'We look stupid. We should be in wetsuits,' Brooke fumed. *Zen*, she reminded herself, breathing deeply the way Maddy had taught her when she was young. *Stay Zen.*

Jack stopped and turned to her, looking at her as if he was surprised she was even there. Arrogant. Self-important. And he still managed to move her…*again*. Annoying.

'Nonsense. It's a beautiful, summer's day in Manly. What you're wearing is perfect. And you all look so good—why would you want to cover that up?'

Jack's eyes were almost black in the sun. His hair was thick, with a slight wave at the front where it swept over as if he'd just run a hand through it. His cheekbones were high and his jaw was strong, but that wasn't what made him sexy. It was the way he looked at her. His chin tilted up, his eyebrows slightly furrowed, his full lips together. Arrogant. Entitled. Confident. As if he was thinking about having sex with her right now.

He stood like a man who was aware of his own presence. He was physically intimidating and he knew it. And he was using that now. Despite the various...*annoying*... movements in her core, Brooke was aware of what he was doing and she wasn't buying into it. He could stand there, all pouty and sexy and as manly as he wanted, but right now all Brooke saw was a snout and two piggy eyes.

'Are you serious? I mean—did you actually *say* that?' Heat rose up the back of Brooke's neck and fizzed in her ears. She turned to the cameraman who was now getting closer to Katy's breasts. 'Did you get that? I mean—on film? Did you get that sexist, disgusting comment on tape?'

She turned back to Jack, who was standing with his hands in his pockets, his face blankly staring at her as if he had no idea what she was talking about.

'Because that's what the Australian public need to see. The extent of this man's sexism and arrogance and...and piggishness.'

Her voice was getting higher. Her fists were in balls. She wasn't even sure what she was saying. But a thought was forming in her head. *That's it!* That was all she had to do! He wouldn't put her on the telly if she was insulting and rude and...and honest! But then if he didn't put her on the telly where would that leave Wright Sports?

Brooke tried to breathe. She tried to think. But her tongue had other ideas. 'This whole show is a vulgar attempt to make women appear shallow and stupid and competitive. A way to prove this man's theory that women are second-class citizens. Well—I won't do it!'

Brooke dropped her surfboard and it made a satisfying thud in the sand.

'And nor will anyone else. Will we, girls?'

Brooke turned to her fellow contestants. Her peeps. Her sisters from other misters. She expected them to crowd around her, fists raised, a cry of *I am woman, hear me roar* on their lips. Just as her real sisters would have. But instead eleven sets of long eyelashes blinked. A seagull swooped and made Contestant Number Four swat above her head. Someone coughed.

'Right, girls?'

The girls were still blinking at her.

'C'mon. We're not going to let him get away with this, are we?'

Someone shuffled in the sand. Katy moved her surfboard from one side to the other.

'We aren't here to be ogled…' Katy said quietly, hesitantly.

'Yes! Exactly!' Brooke let out a yell and pointed at Katy before turning back to Jack. 'We're not here to be ogled. Our *Perfect Match* won't care what we look like. Not if he's truly our perfect match. He won't be attracted to big boobs or a small bum or be interested in the size of our thigh-gap. Love is more chemical than that. Love is more intuitive than that. Our perfect match will see through all that. He'll be attracted to us because of our thoughts, our opinions… That's what we should be showing. Our minds—not our butt cheeks.'

Jack nodded slowly. He pushed his lips together and his mouth turned down at the corners.

'Is that right?' He raised his eyebrows.

'Yes!'

Brooke left her position to move and throw an arm around Katy. Katy was quite a bit taller than Brooke, so putting her arm around her was a little awkward, but they were banding together for a common good. There was nothing awkward about that.

'That's right—isn't it, Katy?'

Katy didn't speak, but she nodded. Slowly. Tentatively. But she definitely nodded.

Brooke squeezed her shoulder. 'We won't be paraded like cattle,' Brooke said firmly.

'Actually…'

Brooke's head swivelled to face Alissa, a blonde-haired, big-boobed beauty who stood behind her.

'I don't mind being in a bikini. I mean—yes—I want my perfect match to want me for who I am, but I mean—a man's got to have a little incentive.' Alissa jiggled her boobs and giggled. 'He *is* a man, after all.'

Brooke watched as the evolution of woman stepped back at least forty years.

'She's right…' another big-bosomed beauty piped up. 'We have to use what we have to attract them in the first place.'

'You don't want a man who's attracted to you just for your looks!' Brooke insisted.

'No,' said someone else. 'But men are men, Brooke. They're visual creatures. They have to like what they see.'

'You're missing the point.' Brooke was feeling hot, and she knew she should probably stop but she couldn't. She needed to say what she had to say. 'Your perfect match will be attracted to *you*. To *your* face and *your* body and *your* eyes—and *your* bum. Not because it's perfect, and not because it's out on display. Think about it—when you're attracted to someone you just *are*. You can't help it. And it doesn't matter if they have a crooked nose or thinning hair. When that chemical attraction takes hold all their imperfections are gorgeous. They make them who they are. You don't see them as negatives—you see everything about them as gorgeous.'

'That's true, Brooke, and I'm not saying we're all perfect. I'm saying that it doesn't hurt to introduce the men to some of our…imperfections.'

Alissa smiled, but Brooke didn't. She turned back to smug Jack Douglas and realised her mistake immediately. He was rocking on his heels with his hands in his pockets. Satisfied. Triumphant.

'And, *cut*!'

Horrified, Brooke turned to face the camera now on her face. Jack sauntered towards her and came in closer than he ever had before, the heat of his skin making her cheeks burn.

'Ratings gold.'

That deep, calm voice didn't calm her this time. But it did make her whole body break out in a rash.

'Good Job, Ms Wright.'

Then he moved back, smiled wide, turned and walked away—while eleven girls stood silently behind her and a lone camera beeped to indicate that it was back on and recording.

CHAPTER THREE

JACK'S HEAD WAS beating incessantly. Over and over. It had started with a throbbing in the back of his head and had now moved to right behind his temple. He resisted the urge to rub at it. All eyes were on him. Now wasn't the time to show any weakness.

'Keep rolling.'

'But, Jack…'

'Keep rolling.'

Jack's calm was slipping. As a matter of fact it was now sliding right out of him and creeping into the ocean, where Contestant Number Three was being hauled up into a lifeboat by three lifeguards. She couldn't swim. A fact she'd failed to mention when they'd told the women they'd be surfing today. So desperate to find her 'perfect match', the crazy woman would rather drown than lose the opportunity to go on a date with a man she'd never met.

Jack tried to relax. The lifeguards had this. But his shoulders stayed tense. He wasn't sure why he was so anxious. Maybe it was the fact that these twelve women were his responsibility. All of them. For the entire six weeks of taping. No matter how much he wanted to stay out of it, the truth was he had to make sure they were safe, make sure they were happy, and make sure they all stayed right where he needed them—in front of the cameras.

Most of them were proving to be easy to manage—except Stephanie Rice, out there, and Ms Wright. The petite blonde. The fiery woman with the sparkling eyes. The woman he couldn't get out of his mind and he suspected the reason his shoulders remained tight even as the lifeguard pulled the flailing contestant out of the water.

Her rousing speech kept going through his mind. Her pink cheeks, her clenched fists. She hadn't just been spouting words back there—she'd felt it. *'When you're attracted to someone you just* are. *You can't help it.'*

He didn't want her to be right about that. She *couldn't* be right about that. It was his responsibility to find perfect matches for these women. But what if she was right?

Attraction *didn't* make sense. It *wasn't* logical. A questionnaire could tell you about likes and dislikes, but it couldn't predict that physical blow right in your chest when you met someone and they blew you away. Not just because of their body or their looks, but because of something else. Something you couldn't explain. Something he was becoming very afraid he felt when he looked at Brooke Wright.

She was a beautiful woman, that was obvious—but it wasn't her beauty that made his heart beat faster when she was around. It was something else. A look she gave him when she was standing up for what she believed in. Attraction was purely physical, wasn't it? Why couldn't he just think about one of the other women? They were beautiful. And they all looked magnificent in a bikini.

But every time he tried to think of another woman his thoughts wandered back to Brooke. To *her* body in that tiny red bikini. To the way she'd tried to rouse the girls. To the way her eyes had glowed brighter and her hair had moved as she'd bounced around, encouraging the girls to fight. Holding her sword aloft against the fire-breathing dragon to protect her people. She was brave and strong and smart and perfect.

But of course she wasn't perfect. She was argumentative and difficult—and if he was honest her mouth was too wide for her face. But somehow that just made him want to look at her even more. He wanted to stare at her and he had to force himself to look away. He was sure he was becoming obvious.

Sex. Lust. That was all it was. Physical attraction. It wasn't as if he hadn't felt it before. He just had to push the feeling down. Easy. He did it all the time. It was just a stupid crush. But somehow it felt different, and that irritated him. She *wasn't* different. She'd be like all the others—after something. His money, his influence, his name. He'd not met anyone yet who liked him for *him*. It was what his father had always warned him about and unfortunately the old man had been right. Every damn time.

He couldn't trust anyone—he knew that. And he definitely couldn't trust Brooke Wright. And not just because he hadn't figured her angle out yet—because she was beginning to occupy his mind a little more than he was comfortable with. And right now he needed to focus on the show. On his father's threats and the executive producer his father was pushing him to take on. And on the contestant they were now struggling to get on an inflatable rescue boat.

He needed to concentrate on how he was going to introduce more twists and turns to keep viewers tuned in. But every time he thought of something he also thought of Brooke's reaction and what she would say. And he wasn't sure why. Why did it even *matter* what she said or did? He barely knew her. She was just another contestant. But the way she'd spoken about the way the show was representing women stuck in his chest. It forced him to think of his mother and the way his father treated her. How he lied to her, cheated on her, threatened her, bullied her. He hated it. He hated seeing the look in her eyes when his father said something cruel or thoughtless or failed to turn up again.

This was nothing like that. This was just a game—just a TV show—surely she could see that? It wasn't real.

But Brooke had no idea. She was too sincere. Too ethical.

Jack ran a hand through his hair. Nothing came easy. Between ensuring this show became a hit, protecting his mother from the truth about his father and trying to earn enough money to buy himself out of his contact, he was wondering when it would let up. When he'd get a break. And now Brooke Wright had come along and embedded herself under his skin. Questioned him. Argued with him. He didn't need that, and he definitely didn't need to feel attracted to her.

He wondered for a minute how someone so small could be so much trouble. And *why* was she so much trouble? The woman seemed constantly angry. Why?

He'd thought he knew all about her. Just as he'd had all the other contestants researched, he'd had *her* researched. Marketing Manager of a family-owned company, one of five sisters. Seemed to have had a comfortable upbringing. Seemed to get along with everyone. No enemies anyone could find. No psycho ex-boyfriends. Currently single. Financially stable.

She had every reason to be perfectly happy, yet clearly she wasn't. At least she wasn't when he was around. Maybe something about *him* made her mad? Maybe he reminded her of an ex-boyfriend or someone else who had annoyed her?

From experience he knew that the way people reacted to each other almost never reflected how they felt about that person—it was more about what was happening in their head. The story they'd made up or the conclusion they'd come to almost never had any bearing on reality. Women were experts at it.

He made a conscious effort to work with facts. Not to read too far into things, to take each moment for what it was. *Don't look forward and don't look back.* So far that approach was working for him, and every time he found himself reflecting or looking forward to something he pushed those feelings right back down where they belonged. Out of sight and out of mind.

Some people called him cold. Distant. One particularly upset woman had called him soulless. But that wasn't true. The truth was everyone had an ulterior motive and you couldn't trust anyone. He was just protecting himself.

The lifeguards' boat had reached the woman in the waves. She was still afloat, waving her arms. Her calls could be heard faintly billowing on the wind as it blew towards shore. His shoulders hurt from holding them so tight but he didn't move his eyes. They had to keep rolling.

He had their number—these women on the show. He knew the ones who were doing it just to get famous, the ones who were looking for true love and the ones who were hoping it would change their lives.

His mind turned back to the Tiny Terror. He wasn't sure what her angle was yet. She seemed sincere when she spoke, but she could just be a very good actress—most women were. She also seemed determined not to spend too much time on-camera. She'd come in, see the camera, smile awkwardly and move towards it, then she'd seem to change her mind and hightail it out of the room, or—more often—give him a tongue-lashing and then leave.

He hadn't figured her out yet, but he would. He always did. Everyone had an angle, and sooner or later they slipped up—giving him the perfect opportunity to see them for what they really were.

'Aren't you going to do anything?'

Jack turned to see the woman he'd just been thinking of. Dripping wet in that small red bikini. It was a *very* small bikini. A bikini that was in danger of exposing even more than it already was. He stood, transfixed. Not by her face but by her body. Her petite but muscular body. It was perfect. It curved in where it should and was soft where there should be softness. But where there was no softness it was hard, glistening with sea water when the sun hit her. His throat went dry and his eyebrows felt heavy.

'She's drowning!'

Her manic cry snapped his head back up to her face. Her forehead was creased and her wide mouth was hanging open. He watched as she drew her bottom lip in and held it against her teeth. His already tense shoulders seized up. She was angry again. Getting ready to tell him off. But rather than annoying him right then it was turning him on.

Not many women argued with him. Not many people in general argued with him. And when they did he could normally talk them down, make a joke and defuse the situation, but she seemed determined to disagree with him. It should annoy the hell out of him, but it didn't. Nothing about her was turning him off right now.

Lust. Physical attraction. That was all this was.

'What?' he asked absently as her lip bounced out from between her teeth again.

'Alissa! She's drowning out there and all you can do is stand and watch.'

Jack's face moved back to the ocean. He remembered Contestant Number Three and the action that was unfolding out on the sapphire-blue water among the white tips of the waves that were crashing relentlessly to the shore.

'She's fine. The lifeguards have her.'

No point panicking. She was in good hands. He hoped she hadn't swallowed too much water. She was a long way out but he could see her moving into the boat. She was flailing about a lot. So much so that one of the lifeguards had just received a nice hefty slap up the side of his head. She was fine.

His shoulders relaxed a little and he allowed a smile to lift one side of his mouth.

'You think this is *funny*?'

Jack felt Brooke move closer. He didn't move a muscle.

'This isn't funny! She could have drowned. She could have died. All for the chance to meet some man she doesn't even know if she's going to like! Don't you see how crazy this is?'

She'd moved now and was standing in front of him. He wished she wasn't. She was angry—that was obvious. He wanted to listen to her and calm her down, but it was hard when she stood dripping in front of him. Her breasts peeped out of her brief bikini top—so much so he was sure that if she just moved a little more he'd be able to see the darkness of her nipple.

'Are you looking at my breasts?'

Busted.

'Yes.' He met her eyes. No point in lying. She'd caught him—and why *wouldn't* he look? They were lovely, and she wasn't exactly trying to cover them up. For someone who had spent an hour arguing about why they should be wearing wetsuits instead of bikinis earlier that morning, she'd chosen herself one of the briefest and sexiest ones he'd ever seen.

'You make me sick.'

'Well, clearly I make you *something*...' He nodded towards her breasts, where her nipples now stood to attention. She was either excited or cold and he didn't mind which. There was something incredibly hot about hard nipples showing through a bikini.

She folded her arms across her chest. 'That—' her voice was practically a hiss '—was caused by extreme anger. At you and your disgusting attitude.'

'In my experience that reaction is usually due to excitement—not anger.'

Her eyes opened wide at that comment, as he'd expected them to do. He was finding annoying her strangely pleasant.

'I can assure you that you *don't* excite me. Quite the opposite. You make me feel...'

She paused and he cocked his head, removing his hands from his pockets to fold them across his chest. How *did* he make her feel? He wanted to know—because right now she was making *him* feel something he hadn't felt in a long time: playful. And interested in what she had to say next.

'I make you feel...what?'

'You make me feel...' Her lips moved as if she was about to say something but nothing came out. 'You make me feel....indignant.'

'Indignant?'

'Yes. And offended and outraged and angry and... and...furious.'

'You seem to be quite an angry person. What's the matter—some old boyfriend do you wrong?'

He could practically light a cigarette with the steam coming out of her ears.

'I am *not* an angry person. I'm actually quite calm and quiet. But you have a way of ruining my Zen.'

'Zen is about inner peace. You need to be at peace with *yourself* to have Zen. It shouldn't matter what other people say and do—other people can't ruin your Zen... only you can do that.'

'Well, apparently you can.'

'I'd love to know what it is exactly that you find so offensive about me. It can't be my looks—I've been told I'm unusually handsome.'

She sniffed and folded her arms, which just resulted in him getting a better view of her breasts. He shifted his eyes quickly.

'And it can't be my personality because—let's face it—I'm charming.' He smiled. She'd laugh at that. Surely? He hadn't seen her laugh and something inside him ached to see her laugh.

But she didn't.

'I find you offensive because you're an insensitive bully who couldn't give a toss about what anyone else thinks.'

For some reason that comment caught in his chest. She'd called him a bully. He *wasn't* a bully. His father was a bully. He wasn't.

'Well, you're an opinionated troublemaker who speaks before thinking. What's the matter—didn't get a say when you were a kid? Picked on by your sisters? Left out? There's got to be a reason you feel this need to stand up for everyone.'

To his surprise, she stopped. Her big eyes widened.

He recognised that look immediately and a foul taste rose in his mouth.

'You really *are* a piece of work, Jack Douglas. You don't care about anyone but yourself, do you? Alissa could have drowned out there and all you can do is stand here on the sand and pass judgement on me when you have no idea who I am.'

Jack sucked in a breath and swallowed.

That look. That was the look his mother's face had when his father let rip with one of his insults. He knew that look and he'd never thought he'd be the one to cause it. He wanted to take it back. He wanted to rewind the tape and start again. But he couldn't, and she was standing there all hurt and confused.

What had he done?

'Brooke...I'm...'

'No.' She stepped back. 'Forget it. I shouldn't have said anything about anything. I shouldn't have expected you of all people to understand what I was trying to say.'

He wanted to stop her from leaving, explain himself, but they were hauling Alissa onto the sand and all he could do was follow Brooke to where the woman lay.

Brooke's body buzzed. Jack Douglas was standing closer to her than he ever had before. Tall and big and confrontational. He was behind her and her breath was coming in short bursts.

What the hell was she *doing*? Why was she getting so emotional? She barely knew this man, but for some reason everything he said seemed to touch her deep down. She wasn't sure what the hell was going on with her lately. She didn't have a bad temper. Not any more. Not for years. Not since she'd been loved and felt loved and had come to realise what it meant to care about people.

She certainly didn't normally lecture people. She was usually the one who stayed well in the background, forced herself to stay in the background—but since she'd been here and since she'd met him she'd felt compelled to stand up. For herself, for the other women, and strangely for all of womankind.

Brooke classed herself as a feminist—surely all self-respecting women did. She believed in equality and didn't appreciate women being treated badly. But she'd never so aggressively attacked someone about their sexism before. But then, she'd never met anyone quite like Jack Douglas. Charming, handsome. A man who took no prisoners. Who used people and spat them out.

Her internet research had proved her suspicions that Jack Douglas was a womanising, partying, poor little rich boy. He worked for his father—had done since leaving his exclusive private school. But what she hadn't found out was any private information. There were plenty of photos of Jack at parties, standing with yet another glamorous woman, but as far as friends or pastimes went the man was impenetrable. It seemed as if he lived alone and was close to no one.

She hated him—she was sure of that. Hated everything he stood for. There really was nothing to like about him. But for some reason her stupid body and her ridiculous mind and her outrageously misinformed heart wouldn't listen.

Lust. Sex. Physical attraction. That was all this was, she reminded herself. Nothing else. He wasn't different from any other handsome man. But somehow it felt different. Awful, dangerous...*different*.

'Ohhh, help me!'

The moan from Alissa brought Brooke back to the moment.

Alissa was coughing and crying and calling out. Her hair was plastered to her face and her bikini was barely staying on her body. She was trying to get up out of the boat, clinging to the shoulders of a lifeguard who was trying to get an oxygen mask on her. But she wouldn't let him.

'I went under...I was drowning...' Her tears were manic, which was clearly making breathing more difficult. She gasped for air and the lifeguard tried to haul her backwards, but she was strong and fought him off, her arms reaching for Jack as he moved past Brooke and knelt at Alissa's side.

'I was going to die out there. I couldn't breathe. I didn't know how to get up!'

Her eyes were wide and tracks of red made them look almost mad. Her hands clawed at Jack's shoulders, soaking his shirt. Brooke saw Jack tense. Something about people touching him clearly made Jack uncomfortable. But he didn't move. He was solid, allowing Alissa to claw at him.

Brooke heard the deep tenor of his voice before she heard his words. Alissa was looking straight into his face, her eyes not moving but her hands still clawing at his shirt.

'You're safe now, Alissa, we have you. You're OK.'

Jack's words were delivered calmly and they reverberated with a sincerity Brooke hadn't heard before.

'C'mon, now, love—you need to lie back. We have to put the mask on.'

'No! No!' Alissa started to move again, away from the lifeguard and closer to Jack and his deep voice.

'It's all right, Alissa. We have you. *I* have you. Just look at me. Look at *me*.'

Alissa turned at his voice and stared into his eyes

again, her gaze shifting from one of his eyes to the other. 'I couldn't breathe.' Tears were falling fast down her face.

Jack let his hand rub from her forehead down the back of her head. 'You're OK now, Alissa. You're safe.'

His calm, steady voice and the way he stroked her head over and over again as his other hand held hers on his shoulder was clearly making Alissa breathe deeply and more steadily. He kept repeating himself, reassuring her, letting her hands claw him until they stilled and her head fell onto his shoulder.

Again Jack tensed. Brooke watched the muscles in his back through the now wet shirt. He didn't move from where he was perched on the sand in front of Alissa. His eyes never left her face.

This was a Jack Brooke hadn't seen before. She hadn't expected it. She hadn't expected the calm with which he handled the situation or the tenderness as he stroked Alissa's head. Jack didn't seem to her to be a sympathetic man. She wondered if he was doing it just for the cameras, but when she looked around the cameras were switched off. This wasn't for TV— this was just him. Calming Alissa down. Making her feel safe.

But of course he was. Anyone would do that in this situation. No one could see a panicked woman and ignore her. He wasn't special. He wasn't doing anything a normal person wouldn't do. Not that she thought him a normal person. But right now, on the beach in the sand, with a woman who'd thought she was going to die, Brooke saw a man. Just a man. Trying to help.

She shook her head. He was the enemy. The man who was trying to make her look like a fool. The man who didn't care about the women on this show. She was just shocked that he was a normal human being, that was all. He definitely wasn't different.

The lifeguard managed to lie Alissa down with Jack's help, but she wouldn't let Jack's hand go. He had to walk to the ambulance with her.

'Please come with me,' begged Alissa, her eyes still red and her chest still heaving.

An ample chest, Brooke noticed. Alissa's breasts were spilling out of her bikini top. Brooke managed to locate a blanket and threw it over Alissa. To keep her warm and protect her modesty. Definitely not because she didn't want Jack to see her breasts. She didn't care whose breasts Jack ogled.

'Of course I will. Brooke—you jump in too.' Jack turned to her for the first time since they'd met Alissa on the beach.

'Me? What for? There's not enough room.' It wasn't that she didn't want to go with Alissa. She just didn't like to be ordered about by him. And she noticed the cameras had been turned on again.

'Because I shouldn't be in the shots and she needs someone to be with her the whole time. You'll have to sit next to her so it looks like you're taking her to the hospital.'

Brooke wanted to argue. She wanted to tell him that it wasn't reality TV if he dictated who went where and sat where and said what—where was the reality in that? But the truth was she was worried about Alissa and she knew Alissa wouldn't let him go. And she knew he'd keep insisting and she just wanted to fix this.

So she hauled herself up into the ambulance, knowing the camera was on her face and knowing it would look as if she was the one who was comforting Alissa when it was really Jack.

But then she remembered her tiny red bikini. And how good it would look if she were the heroine, helping someone in her Wright Sports bikini. And she thought of her sisters, and she sat in the ambulance and held Alissa's hand while Jack sat on the other side, just out of camera view, doing all the comforting work.

CHAPTER FOUR

THE OXYGEN AND whatever else the lifeguards and the paramedics had mixed into Alissa's mask was calming her down. They'd checked her out and there didn't seem to be anything very wrong with her. Her lungs had taken in a lot of water and she was in shock, but otherwise she was well. No cuts or bruises or dangerous internal injuries.

Alissa's hand relaxed in Brooke's. Her eyes rolled back and forth between Brooke and Jack.

'You saved me,' she said to Jack, who was off-camera.

He smiled at her. Brooke watched his face as the sincere smile softened it. Lines appeared at his eyes. He looked older, gentler. More real. He didn't say anything but flicked his eyes suddenly to Brooke and raised his eyebrows—nodding as if to tell her to say something in response because he wasn't supposed to be there.

'Oh, you're...you're safe now, Alissa.'

Alissa's head lolled back to Brooke. 'Brooke, you're here too?' She was smiling.

Brooke smiled back and squeezed the spaced-out Alissa's hand. 'I'm here too.'

'You're here... You're always here. Fighting for us and sticking up for us and not taking any crap from anyone. Our big sister.'

Alissa squeezed Brooke's hand and tried to get up. Brooke rested her hand on Alissa's shoulder. Jack did the same on his side.

'You're so little, but you're so big—y'know? Angry. Loud. Opinionated.'

Alissa smiled at her and Brooke smiled tightly back. Brooke knew Alissa's drugs were starting to kick in, but her words had still managed to freeze Brooke's heart. Angry? Loud? Opinionated? *Her?* Was that what they thought of her? That *so* wasn't her. Quiet. Predictable. Dull. Easy. That was her. Happy. Alissa was just pumped up on something. She didn't know what she was talking about.

'I'm not loud...' Brooke's eyes flicked to Jack's and they met. He smiled with one side of his mouth and she understood. She was *always* loud with him. And angry and argumentative. This was bad. This show was changing her. She was becoming someone she wasn't and she didn't like it.

'We've been worried about you, Brooke...' Alissa was talking again—all slurred and sleepy. 'Who's going to be your perfect match? What man will want you? You'll frighten them all away with your angry women's lib speeches and all those little muscles you have. So *hard*, Brooke...' Alissa reached out and squeezed Brooke's bicep. 'Hard and angry.'

Brooke's smile froze. That was what the others thought of her? That wasn't her. She wasn't hard or angry. It was these cameras and Jack. Brooke looked up. *Him.* It was him who brought this out in her. This side of her personality she thought she'd buried years ago.

'You're pretty, though. You have a lovely smile. You should smile more. You'd look prettier. And you have some amazing clothes!' Alissa turned to Jack. 'She's pretty and nice and has nice clothes. You like her, don't you, Jack? *He* likes you Brooke. Can't stop looking at you. Can you, Jack? Maybe *he's* your perfect match!'

Brooke knew it was the drugs talking. She knew Alissa had no idea what she was saying. But still her words made her stop still. Jack *looked* at her? No, he didn't. Not like that. He thought she was a troublemaker. Someone who spoke without thinking. He didn't like her.

A lump caught in Brooke's chest. She'd thought her temper was gone. Her sisters had made sure of that. They'd loved her despite her temper. But her parents hadn't been able to tolerate it. She hadn't been good enough for them.

The thought flew into her head unexpectedly. She hadn't thought like that in years. Her sisters had made sure those thoughts stayed out of her head. But her sisters weren't here. She hadn't seen them or talked to them in almost a week and she just wasn't herself without them. She was angry and volatile and now she was pathetic and feeling sorry for herself.

Right now, as she held Alissa's hand and let the drugged woman's words swirl in her head, all she wanted to do was call her sisters. But Jack's rules stated that there was to be no contact with the outside world. The only people they could talk to were people on the show.

Jack had provided counsellors, and a couple of the girls had already spoken to them. But Brooke just wanted her sisters. The women who loved her and cared about her and wanted the best for her. The people who would tell her when she was being difficult, let her know when her dress was too short and hold her when everything got too much. But they weren't here and the cameras were rolling and Alissa was still going on to Jack about how much he looked at Brooke.

'No one is looking at me, Alissa. You're right. I'm too loud and angry. But I'm not worried about me right now—how are *you* feeling?'

Alissa moved sluggishly. 'Oh, darling, you're not angry at me, are you?' Alissa turned to Jack. 'She's always angry at something and someone. Mainly you. Why is she so angry at you all the time? What have you done? Have you hurt her?' Alissa tried to get up again. 'Don't you hurt her—because she sticks up for us and she's good and kind and lovely and I don't *want* you to hurt her.'

Brooke's cheeks burned. Alissa's words were making it more and more awkward by the second. Her insistence that Jack felt something for her was ridiculous. And her insistence that Brooke was an angry person was even more humiliating. Angry was something she never wanted to be again.

Brooke couldn't look at Jack. She knew what she'd see. Horror. Denial. She had to get Alissa to stop talking about her because the cameras were rolling and she wouldn't shut up and she didn't want everyone in Australia hearing about all this stuff.

'You need to rest, Alissa. Stop talking and rest.'

Finally she looked at Jack. She dreaded his smug and patronising face. Or, worse, his pathetic sad face, feeling sorry for her. But when she looked at him his face was none of those things. He was looking at her, his eyes steady and his jaw set. He looked as if he wanted to say something, but he didn't. He just held her eyes as he held Alissa's hand.

Alissa spoke again, this time to Jack, but Brooke didn't hear. All she could focus on was Jack's direct look. It spoke of comfort and understanding and resolution. She wasn't sure why, but he was holding her gaze steady.

Brooke felt the thumping in her chest caused by Alissa's words starting to recede. Alissa was talking about something else now. Something about a zoo and the animals escaping. Her words made Brooke break Jack's gaze and she looked back just in time to see Alissa start to doze off.

The paramedics came then and checked her over, so Brooke moved away to the front of the ambulance. She watched as the camera followed the movements of the paramedics and Alissa, and didn't notice that Jack had moved and was now sitting next to her.

'I think she'll be OK.'

He didn't say anything about what Alissa had said. Good. She didn't want him to.

'You look at me?' *No, don't say that.*

'I...'

'You hate me.'

'I don't hate you, Brooke.'

'You said I was a troublemaker.'

'You are.'

'Then why do you look at me?' Brooke faced him, her fingers hurting as she gripped the seat. She really shouldn't be talking—shouldn't be asking him this. Why couldn't she just shut up?

His dark eyes held hers. Brooke's heart thumped. They weren't close. They weren't touching. But she could feel him. Feel him breathing and feel him near her. Big and strong and solid. She held her breath.

'I look at you because I find it hard to turn away.'

Brooke sat silently. She had nothing to say. No words formed on her tongue or in her head. Nothing.

Alissa started to talk again and the ambulance bounced heavily on the road. Brooke felt Jack's leg press against hers. Deliberately. It didn't move with the bumps. The muscles in his thigh were tense. He was keeping his leg right next to hers.

Again, he'd surprised her. What the hell was going on and why was her heart beating so fast? What did she care if he looked at her? If he couldn't turn away? She didn't want his attention. She didn't want *him*. So why did his words seep so quickly and violently into her dry, parched heart?

'I'm not normally angry. Or opinionated.'

Why had she said that? She didn't have to justify herself to him.

'It's OK to be angry sometimes. If you don't like something you should speak up. This situation you're in would make anyone angry.'

'I'm not me right now. You don't even know me.'

He smiled and the ambulance moved again, rocking her sideways. Although she wasn't entirely sure the ambulance had moved…

'You're right. I don't know you. But I do know you're more than angry. You're loyal and passionate and…you're gorgeous.'

'Gorgeous?'

She kept her eyes on him and his eyes remained on her. He held steady with every bump and every turn and she involuntarily leaned a little closer, mesmerised by the way he held her still.

'Stunning.'

His words were sincere and his voice was deep, and the way he said it—not looking away as his body held against her still—made something shake inside her. A feeling she knew lay dormant—something she didn't want to wake—stirred. She pushed it down, but it rattled her as he looked at her.

'What's so stunning about me?'

Her voice was quiet but she wanted to know. She really wanted to know what he could possibly find stunning about her. She wasn't that pretty. And since she'd met him she'd abused him and caused him trouble and been mean and rude and difficult and so angry. How did he find *that* stunning?

She waited for his answer. Not breathing, not moving—allowing the moment to last.

'Everything.'

His answer came just as the ambulance pulled up at the hospital. A mad rush meant everyone was pulled out of the ambulance and the cameras rushed to film their responses. Brooke was whisked away by one of the production staff and Jack remained at the ambulance.

Brooke's heart beat hard and fast. Adrenalin rushed through her. *Everything.* That was what he'd said. Everything? How could he say that? What did he mean? He didn't even know her. And what he did know wasn't very good. Why had he said that? Was it a line? He'd seemed so sincere.

Confusion rattled her brain and made her reactions slow.

'We've got to get you to the emergency beds, Brooke. We want you to go see Alissa.'

The production team rushed her to Alissa's side. Jack didn't reappear.

Brooke spent the afternoon getting ice and water and food for Alissa. She didn't see Jack again but she did think about him. *A lot.* He'd said that everything about her was stunning. Was that what he really thought?

Confusion made her tired. Alissa's demands made her tired. Until eventually she fell asleep on a hospital chair, dressed in nothing but a bikini and dreaming of drowning in a sea of crashing waves.

CHAPTER FIVE

BOTH THE GIRLS were asleep. Heavy breathing and the occasional snore coming from under the covers in the bed assured Jack that Alissa was sleeping soundly, and Brooke was on an armchair, her head bent right over to the arm, her legs twisted.

She looked uncomfortable, but she was asleep too. Deep, steady breaths came from her tiny body. She was still and quiet—two things he'd never associated with her. Brooke was a fireball of energy and opinions. She made him tense, but yesterday in the ambulance he'd seen something else in her. A vulnerability he'd not noticed before.

Alissa's words had shocked and upset her and he'd known exactly what Brooke was feeling. She hadn't had to tell him—he'd been able to see it in the way her shoulders had fallen forward. In the way her eyes had opened and she'd sucked the edge of her bottom lip in. Alissa had hurt her.

For a moment Brooke hadn't looked like a confident woman. She'd looked like a little girl bullied in the schoolyard. Unsure how to react. That was why he'd felt the need to come to her rescue. Feeling alone and picked on was a feeling he knew too well. He didn't deserve to feel that way and neither did Brooke.

He'd wanted to tell her that Alissa didn't know what she was talking about. He'd wanted her to know that having cameras pointed in her face and feeling out of control was normal—and so was her reaction. Getting angry wasn't a weakness—sometimes it was the right thing to do. But clearly she wasn't comfortable with that side of her personality. Something about losing control upset Brooke, and he wanted to find out why. He wanted to know more.

But he shouldn't have said what he had. Brooke might think things. She might imagine he wanted something he didn't and he didn't want her to do that. Because he didn't want anything. He couldn't allow anything to happen—and not only for the sake of the show. He knew that if he let Brooke in he would hurt her for sure.

Brooke was the kind of woman who threw herself into things. A defender of the universe. A superwoman. Strong and kind. But she was still a woman. She still got hurt. Alissa had hurt her. And he knew he would hurt her too. At the beach, he'd said things he didn't mean. As much as he tried to keep it at bay he knew deep down he was just like his father. A selfish bastard who was only out for himself.

Today he'd fix it. He'd let her know what he'd meant. She *was* gorgeous, of course—she was passionate and interesting and argumentative and challenging and a breath of fresh air. She'd be special to someone one day. Someone would see her and sweep her off her feet and they'd deserve her. But it wouldn't be him.

Brooke moved and moaned and shifted, and sleepily she opened her eyes. Rubbing them, she ran her fingers through her hair and yawned wide as she sat up, looking around. He could see she was a little confused and unsure where she was.

'Good morning, Sleeping Beauty.' Best to keep it light and flirty.

She turned to him with a start. 'Jack! What are you doing here?'

'Just checking on the patient.'

Her eyes darted behind him. They opened wide and narrowed. 'You brought the cameras?'

'Of course.' Brooke seemed constantly surprised by the appearance of the cameras. Didn't she know what she'd signed up for?

'Jack, Alissa is going to wake up and feel terrible. She's going to *look* terrible. She's not going to want the cameras here.'

Brooke was sitting up now. All quiet and peace was fast evaporating. Jack's shoulders tensed. Ready for a fight. Brooke liked to fight with him, it seemed. She did it so often. He wondered for a moment what she'd be like if she didn't want to fight. All soft and loving, lying in his bed after a wild session.

His mind wandered...he grew hard. Taming Brooke would be a fun task. She was certainly hot—and he was sure she'd be the type to demand she received her own pleasure in bed. He wasn't into those girls who just lay there—waiting for him to take what he wanted. He liked a bit of spit and fire in the bedroom. He liked a fight—it made the winning so much sweeter.

What he *didn't* like was the cuddling afterwards. Most women liked to cuddle—they wanted to snuggle and touch. But he liked to get up and away. Not because he didn't feel affection for the women but because touching seemed a little too personal, a little too close. He wasn't into close. And he suspected Brooke was the kind of woman who needed close.

'Jack.'

Brooke's angry tone brought him back to the hospital room. Brooke's long-sleeved shirt was open, revealing a tight white singlet. He'd had someone go to the house and get some clothes for the girls last night. They couldn't stay in their swimsuits. Jack's mind wandered back to Brooke's red bikini. It hadn't left much to the imagination. And her body was perfect. Small, tight and athletic. Strong. He imagined how athletic she'd be in bed.

'Jack.'

Again her voice brought him back and his eyes turned to hers. She was angry now. Clearly she didn't like being ignored. 'You need to send the cameras away until she wakes and fixes herself up.'

No. He didn't. The whole point was to see real reactions. The audience would love to see these two, just woken up after a night in hospital. But Brooke was right—no one would want a camera in their face right after they woke.

'This is what you both signed up for, Brooke—Alissa knows that.'

'Alissa had no idea she was going to end up in hospital. I'm sure she didn't sign up for *that*.'

'The cameras are staying.'

He was done arguing. The more she talked, the more sense she made—and he didn't want to change his mind. He knew what would rate best and he needed this show to work, so he didn't want her changing his mind. He couldn't modify this show—not for her or anyone else. It had to be raw and real and make people sit up and take notice.

'What do you care, anyway? You look great. And it'll make you look good to be here when she wakes up— people will love you.'

He knew he'd said the wrong thing even before he'd

finished his sentence. She stood up. White-hot rage seeped through her eyeballs at him. Her fists clenched and her shirt slipped off her shoulder but she was too mad to fix it. His eyes moved to the golden tan of her shoulder. Smooth, with a smattering of freckles from too much time in the sun.

'I don't care how people see me, Jack. This isn't about me—or you, for that matter. This is about Alissa and the fact that she almost died yesterday. Do you even *get* that? Or do you just think about ratings and audiences and everything else that doesn't matter?'

'That's *all* that matters right now, Brooke.'

Didn't she get that? Why couldn't she understand that this wasn't about her or Alissa? This was about making good TV.

'No, it's not what matters. You're so caught up in what people think that you forget what this is really about. Twelve women so disillusioned with love that they think coming on some badly conceived TV show will help them find it. I don't care what you think—that's what these girls are here for—to find love. Not be made fools of in front of the nation.'

'These girls are here to get their heads on the TV. If they weren't they'd find some other way to find love.'

'No. The problem is people like you, Jack. People who perpetrate the myth that men fall in love with looks. But they don't. There's plenty of beautiful women out there, but true love is not about what you look like on the telly or on Instagram or on Facebook. It's not about what people think about you, it's about who you actually are. It's about the type of person you are and the little things that someone notices. People aren't attracted to a perfect nose or the right shade of blonde in your hair. It's not that specific. You can't explain why you're attracted to some people but not others. These women think that if they look hot and do some cool things they'll be desirable, but that kind of attention attracts meat-heads and pathetic, insecure men who don't want a real women—they want the image of a woman. And those are the men these girls should be staying away from.'

She was right. This *wasn't* the place to find a decent bloke. This was a television show. Even though it was called reality it wasn't—you didn't live your life on a TV screen. But right now she seemed to be blaming him for the wrongs of the world. Putting everything that was wrong with society and modern dating on him. It wasn't his responsibility to make these women see themselves as more than just images. It was his job to deliver a TV show that would achieve high ratings. That was it. The end of his responsibility.

'They're all over eighteen—they can make their own minds up.'

'You have no idea, do you? Have you ever stopped to think of what goes on in the lives of these women outside this show? Do you even know anything about them? They could have no support. They could have a group of family and friends who make them feel less than they are. Have you ever thought about the reasons they're here?'

'No!'

That had come out louder than he'd wanted. But she was making him feel things he didn't want to feel. Like guilt. Why should he feel guilty? He hadn't begged these women to come on the show. He wasn't responsible. He couldn't be responsible. That just led to trouble and he couldn't afford trouble. Not this time.

CHAPTER SIX

BROOKE HAD STOPPED talking. She was clearly surprised by his violent outburst. Good. He needed her to be quiet. He needed to think. Or not think in this case. He just needed this to happen.

'Mick, get the boys in here. We need to start taping.' Alissa was waking. He needed her reaction. He needed to get out of the way so the scene could get shot.

He stepped back, away from Brooke and out of the way, but Brooke stepped forward.

'Don't you leave. You want people to see the real reactions then you need to be here. You need to take responsibility. You were a big part of this—you sent Alissa into the ocean, you calmed her down, and I suspect you were the one to send all the clothes and supplies for us. Now you're here. You need to be in this, too.'

No, he didn't. 'I'm not on the show—you are. Now turn around and talk to your friend.'

He was sure that order would send her into a fit. He was sure that would make great TV and he was sure he only felt a slight twitch at the thought of that. But she didn't have a fit. She smiled. She looked at him, direct and hot in the eye. Then she turned and went to Alissa.

It took half an hour of Brooke talking to remind Alissa of where she was and what had happened. Alissa delivered a magnificent performance, forgetting where she was and then crying over the accident before declaring that she hoped her perfect match was worth the trouble. Perfect line. Perfect TV. But for some reason it didn't make Jack feel good. It made him feel old and jaded and uncomfortable. Uncomfortable because he knew he'd just done something his father would have been proud of.

The food in the hospital was terrible. Brooke pushed the plate away and it scraped noisily, echoing in the empty space. Brooke's neck ached and her shoulders hurt. A night spent sleeping upright in a chair had taken its toll. Especially after a day surfing and hours consoling Alissa, who was clearly OK but still sore and unsteady.

And the cameras wouldn't go away. They captured every word and every movement and Brooke was sure she looked about as cute as she did after a particularly hard workout. All she wanted to do was go home and have a shower and sleep. But she couldn't. Because Jack always wanted another shot, and the cameramen were always wanting her to sit and look this way or that.

The more Brooke saw of it, the more she realised there *was* no reality in reality TV. The reality was behind the camera. The reality was Jack. The man who said she was stunning. The man she couldn't stop thinking about.

What had he meant yesterday? Why had he told her everything about her was stunning? It made it so hard to stay angry with him. He made bad choices. He did things for the wrong reasons. But this show wasn't her responsibility and neither were the other eleven women. All she had to do was wear Wright Sports gear and get Wright Sports products on prime-time TV.

She needed to calm down. Maybe it was just the lack of sleep and the fact that it had been almost eight days since she'd had any contact with her sisters that was making her so angry. Brooke breathed deeply. Where the hell was her Zen?

'Here you are.'

Jack. Again. Brooke searched for the cameras. She was sick of them. Sick of watching what she said and thinking about how she looked. She just wanted a minute to herself—which was why she was down here in the hospital canteen.

'Jack. Seriously. I can't do this right now. I'm exhausted. I can't do cameras.' She was too tired to fight. She just needed him and his annoying cameras to go away.

'There are no cameras.'

Brooke looked up in surprise.

'I wanted to talk to you in private.'

In private? Jack never did anything in private. He was all about the show. Brooke was immediately nervous. He wasn't going to say she was stunning again, was he? Because she didn't know what he meant by that…and it was probably just a line…and he was probably lying to get his own way…and that would make her angry and she really didn't want to get angry again.

'What about?'

'About before.' Jack scraped back a plastic chair and the noise reverberated across the vacant canteen.

'Before?'

'Before. In Alissa's room.'

'Jack. I can't fight right now. I'm too tired.'

She *was* tired. Tired of Alissa's complaining and tired of being constantly watched and tired of this bad, bitter coffee. She put the cup down and made to stand, but Jack's arm on hers stopped her. That made her still. Jack rarely touched her. Not voluntarily. She'd noticed that about him. He didn't touch anyone and he stood well away from people. The couple of times she'd accidentally touched him he'd actually flinched.

'I'm not here to fight, Brooke. I'm here to apologise.'

That stopped her. Jack? Apologising? That just didn't seem right. Something about it didn't compute.

'You are?'

'I was an ass before. I made you do something you didn't want to do. I should have waited until you girls were awake and ready before I brought those cameras in there.'

Brooke sat heavily. Jack's apology stilled her tongue. She didn't know what to say. She'd never heard him say he was sorry—he didn't seem the type of person ever to apologise. This man had a real knack for confusing her.

'Brooke?'

'You're saying sorry?'

'Yes.'

'You're saying I was right?'

He paused. His mouth went tight, then his dark eyes set on hers. 'Yes.'

Yes. He was admitting she was right.

The shock was too much. She was tired and surprised and Brooke didn't know what else to do so she leaned forward and rested her head on her hands.

'Brooke?'

She felt Jack's hand on her arm. It was warm and he squeezed her firmly. She sat up quickly and grabbed his hand, squeezing back. Jack's face registered shock and he tried to pull away, but she didn't let him. He wasn't getting away that easily.

'You're sorry? You think I'm right? You're taking responsibility?'

'Yes.'

Brooke let her fingers lace between his and he tried to pull away again. Again she didn't let him. She just pulled her light plastic chair closer to him. So close their knees were touching.

'Where is Jack? What have you done with him?' she teased.

She knew he wanted to pull away, she knew she was making him uncomfortable, and she liked the power she had over him. But he didn't pull away. He actually smiled at her joke and leaned in closer. Brooke noticed his skin. It was dark and smooth and a sprinkling of hairs spread across his jaw, as if he hadn't shaved that morning. He looked a little dishevelled. He looked a little less than the put-together, in control Jack she knew. She liked it. It made him more real somehow.

She leaned closer, taking in his eyes, dark and dancing. His mouth had turned up at the edges. She watched it, then watched his eyes again. They were exploring her face. She suspected he was trying to figure out what she was doing and what she was thinking. She pulled on his hand, letting it rest on her chest. She liked it there. She liked this Jack. The Jack without the Instagram filter.

'I've got him locked up somewhere you'll never find him.'

'Good!' She laughed. 'Keep him there—I prefer this Jack.'

'Why?'

'Because he's real. He feels things. He touches me.'

Jack's smile disappeared. She felt his fingers tighten over hers. 'You like it when I touch you?'

'Yes. Very much. I like your hands. I like your fingers.'

She squeezed his fingers again, before letting go and allowing her own fingers to trail over his palm. When she looked up he was watching her fingers. Brooke's breathing became shallow. In this moment this wasn't Jack. In her sleep-deprived, hungry state this seemed to be someone else. Someone sincere and real whose warm hands she wanted to feel on her skin. Someone who thought she was stunning.

Jack's eyes met hers. Their stare was unbroken—both were having trouble breathing. Brooke wasn't sure if it was the lack of sleep or the gratefulness she felt for his physical touch, but that was what she blamed when she leaned forward and let her lips rest gently on his.

Jack didn't move. He didn't react. He let her press her lips to his and sat still, clinging to her fingers. Brooke opened her eyes, instantly regretting what she'd done. He still didn't move. Except his eyes. They darted from one of hers to the other, but he didn't pull away. Did he want her to do it again? His hand still clung to hers. Should she kiss him again?

She didn't know what to do so she kissed him again. And this time he did react. He pushed closer. He kissed her back, his tongue pushing on her lips till they opened, letting him in. He still didn't let go of her hand and it was hot in hers. His lips were hot too as he tilted his head so his kisses could deepen.

Brooke's heart pounded in her chest. The kiss felt wrong and forbidden. It was over in seconds, and it left her breathless and a little shocked and a lot embarrassed. She let go of his hand and sat back. She blinked, unsure as to why the hell she'd done that.

Brooke couldn't speak but she looked at his face, wondering what he was thinking. He looked back at her blankly before a slow smile spread over his face. A slow, knowing smile that made Brooke's heart drop.

'Nice kiss.'

Brooke shut her eyes tight. *Nice kiss.* That was all it was. He didn't feel anything. He'd just taken the opportunity. He hadn't been kissing her back. He'd just been kissing whoever kissed him. She was right about him—a total player. Incapable of real feelings. Despite his apology. Despite his 'stunning' comment. Of *course* he didn't really think she was someone special. She needed to stop doing that. Stop thinking that people meant what they said and that their actions meant anything. All that kiss meant was that she was tired and he would kiss anyone, anywhere.

Totally disappointed in herself, and extremely over it, Brooke stood.

'That was a bad idea.'

Jack stood as well, his smile now gone. 'Was it?'

'Yes. Very bad. I need to go.'

'Wait.'

Brooke turned back, stupid hope lifting her heart. 'What?'

'I came down here to talk to you. I wanted to ask you something.'

So that was it. He was only apologising because he wanted something. She was so naïve sometimes.

'What?'

'Meet me tonight at Lottie's, near the apartment. For a drink.'

Jack sat back, his eyes blank and his jaw tight again. Gone was friendly, affectionate Jack from moments back. Uncaring, unfeeling, business Jack had escaped from his ropes and was back. He wanted something. Not just a drink—something else. Brooke was sure of it. A hot rash spread up Brooke's neck and into her cheeks. Embarrassment—that was what she felt right now. She was embarrassed that she'd managed to let herself be played by a man she knew was a player. God, she must be tired!

'I'm not sure that's a good idea.'

Jack paused. He sat back even further.

'I mean, clearly we just broke some kind of contestant/producer ethical code or something. I shouldn't have done that.'

A slight vulnerability shadowed his dark eyes. Brooke's heart saw it before her eyes did. Did he actually *want* to take her for a drink? No. *No.* He wanted something. Information. Maybe he wanted to tape her getting sloshed. He definitely didn't want to take her for a drink because he felt something, otherwise he would have said something other than 'nice kiss'.

Brooke's stomach swirled and her head hurt. She wanted him to take her for a drink because he felt the attraction she did. She wanted him to take her for a drink so they could get to know each other, without the cameras and the lights and the direction. She wanted him to feel something—but she wasn't sure he was capable of that. Not with his aversion to closeness and his playboy reputation.

Brooke wanted to get out—away from him and his knowing eyes and his expert lips and the way he was making her move again. Move violently. She didn't want to feel for him. She just wanted to go home and sleep and forget about her recent lapse in judgement.

'But you did, and we should probably talk about it.'

'No, we shouldn't.' Brooke stood to leave.

'Brooke, I know why you're here. For your family's business. I've noticed that you wear Wright Sports clothing most of the time.'

Brooke watched his face. Was he angry? Did that mean he wanted her off the show? For some reason that didn't make her as happy as she'd thought it would. She didn't like the way this show was changing her, the fact that it was making her angry and aggressive, but she liked the other girls. And who would stand up for them against Jack and his outrageous demands if she wasn't there? He'd apologised to her just minutes ago—maybe she was getting through to him. What if she left and he just went back to his old ways?

'What…what are you going to do about it?'

'Nothing. If you come and have a drink with me.'

Brooke wanted to have a drink with him. She wanted to be alone with him. But she wasn't sure if that was such a great idea. Maddy had said this show would be good for her, that it would take her out of her comfort zone. Having a drink with bad-boy Jack Douglas was certainly that. Maybe she should do it.

'Will the cameras be there?'

'No!' he answered emphatically. 'No. It'll just be me and you.'

Her and him. And a drink. In a dark bar. This was dangerous, and so out of her comfort zone. But she wanted to do it. That kiss had made her feel something she hadn't felt in so long. Alive. Excited. No longer numb. Maybe this was just what she needed.

'I'll send someone to pick you up. You might get lost.'

'I don't need an escort and I never get lost.'

Brooke still wasn't sure if this was a good idea. She still didn't know what he wanted or how he felt, and she certainly didn't want any witnesses. No cameras, no one else. Just him and her.

'No, I bet a good girl like you always checks Google Maps.'

'That's right. I'm good, but when people screw with me I can get very bad.' She wasn't sure of that, but it annoyed her that he'd pegged her as a good girl. She'd been bad before. He had no idea.

Another lazy smile spread across his face. He slipped his hands into his pockets. 'Good girl gone bad? I'm looking forward to that.'

Brooke didn't say anything. He didn't deserve any more of her time and he looked too hot right now, all crumpled and lazily sexy, so she turned and left. Before any more bad thoughts could creep their way into her good head.

CHAPTER SEVEN

THE NIGHT WAS hot and still. Laughs rang out from the restaurants that lined the footpath. The smell of the sea lingered in the air and Brooke breathed it in.

Brooke had spent almost her whole life living in Sydney, but she'd never spent much time in Manly. Her family lived in the inner west and she worked in the city and there just weren't that many reasons to cross the bridge. But she liked it. She liked the laidback, casual charm of the coastal suburb. She liked the feeling that it was trapped in holiday mode. No one seemed to work in Manly—they just went to the beach and jogged with their dogs.

But she was missing her sisters and she was missing her work. The *Perfect Match* contract said they were to have no contact with anyone other than each other for the six weeks of taping. No internet, no smartphone. Which was harder than it sounded.

Although Brooke got along with the girls, she missed the comfortable ease of having her sisters on hand. It had been eight days now that they'd been holed up in the penthouse and, although the days had been filled with briefings and hair and make-up sessions and various staged tapings, Brooke was starting to feel very anxious and a little lost without her sisters.

Lottie's was one of those new Sydney bars. One of those discreet hole-in-the-wall places with almost no signage at the front—because signage was, like, *so* five years ago. It took Brooke a few laps around the Corso to find it. She almost wished she'd taken Jack up on his offer of an escort, but the more she thought about it the more she thought the escort would have been a spy.

She didn't know what to make of Jack. He was so confusing and he made her so angry. All she wanted to do was go back to the way things had been. Predictable. Easy. Dull. *Dull?* Where had *that* thought sprung from? Her life wasn't dull. She had her sisters and her friends and she had fun.

But as her heels clicked on the cobblestones she was remembering how she'd felt before she'd come on this hideous show. Numb. But she didn't feel numb any more. She felt anything but numb. She was on some mad, out-of-control rollercoaster and she was sure she wanted to get off. She had to concentrate on not letting her emotions get away from her and on not getting angry. And she had to concentrate very hard on not letting Jack get under her skin.

But as she slipped through the heavy wooden door and spotted Jack in the corner, sipping on a short glass of something dark, her focus went out of the window.

In the darkness of the bar, with the slow sexy beat of the music in the background, Jack was looking…delicious. There was no other word. This wasn't work Jack— this was night-time Jack. And all those rumours about all those women suddenly became so much more believable. He had on a dark shirt, open at the neck but not too far so as to seem sleazy. As she got closer she noticed his black pants were pulled tight at his knees to expose some very nicely developed vastus lateralis muscles. She'd been trying to develop those muscles for two years, but her knees were still knobbly and the muscles there pathetically small. His were anything but small. Hard, muscular thighs.

He saw her and smiled and she steeled herself against the anxious flutter in her chest.

Don't look at his smile, look at his teeth. White, straight—perfect. *No, not helping. Look away.*

His hair. Look up. It looked thick and wavy and he was holding it up over his forehead. Very nice hair. *Don't look at his hair.*

His eyes. Dark and velvety. Chocolaty. Sexy. Bedroom eyes. *Definitely don't look there.* Especially not now he'd said she was gorgeous. Stunning. She remembered the way he'd said it. The word had rolled off his tongue like a thick, sticky liquor and she'd become stuck in it. Even now the word stuck in her head and wouldn't get out.

A lazy layer of dark stubble sat on his jaw. Good— she preferred clean-shaven. Except on him… She liked the stubble. She didn't want to but she did. It made him look a little rougher, a little more manly—maybe even a little dirty.

Oh, crap.

Movement rattled her core. Annoying hot, sexual movement. She tried to force it away but it swelled and intensified—as did her confusion about Jack and what she was feeling about him. She wasn't into all that He-Man stuff. Sensitive. Caring. That was what she liked. Stubble was not her thing. *He* was not her thing.

Focus on something else. His hands. They were resting on his knees as he sat in that wildly confident way some men did. Knees apart. On show. Boasting. *No! Don't look there.*

Concentrate. His hands. His fingers were long and his

hands looked solid. As if they'd never let go. She imagined he'd have a great grip for rope climbs. She wondered if he worked out. He raised his hand to wave and his shirt pulled at his shoulder. Yep. Definitely worked out. So definitely not her type.

Brooke swallowed hard and pulled at the collar of her shirt. She'd undone a few buttons so her bra just peeked out. She'd wanted to look sophisticated, in charge and in control. But now all she felt was exposed. She tried to cover herself up a little before pushing her lips into a wide smile and attempting to saunter towards him.

He didn't get up. Bad, *bad* man. He just smiled and said, 'You look incredibly sexy tonight. Hot date?'

Thank God it was dark, because a hot blush spread up Brooke's neck and into her cheeks. Of *course* he'd think she'd dressed provocatively for him. For him to enjoy. But that wasn't why she'd done it. She'd wanted to look like a woman in charge—she'd wanted to look stunning.

'No. I'm meeting an arrogant player who thinks he can win me over with a few free drinks.'

He smiled. Slow and sexy. And lust licked up around Brooke's body.

'Well, if I see him I'll get rid of him, because I want you all to myself tonight.'

Brooke stopped. What was *that*? A line? She didn't want a line. Anger mingled with the lust and her lust for him made her angry. Brooke felt her emotions bubble to the surface again. Nope. Zen didn't exist when she was around Jack. She needed to fix this. She needed to find out why he made her so angry. Tonight. She had to stop this and go back to the way things had been. However dull that was. She couldn't keep getting angry. Anger never solved anything.

'Jack, why am I here? What do you want?'

He turned his head and smiled at her. One of his fake smiles she was so used to.

'Why do you assume I want something?'

'You think it's amateur hour? I know all about you. I know the kinds of things you get up to.'

'Sounds like you Googled me. You're someone who graduated with a high distinction in marketing and business management—I would have thought your research abilities were better than that.'

'I can do more than use Google, Jack. You'd be surprised at the things I manage to dig up about people.'

'Would I? You graduated in the top ten per cent of the state six years ago, then studied at uni by distance because you started working for the family business the day after you left school. One of five highly competitive and athletic sisters. Mother Mandy, a former Commonwealth hurdler, and father Mark, head coach at the Australian Institute of Sport. You run marketing for the company, which has a current annual turnover of almost a million dollars—a turnover that is mostly due to your sisters' bravery and your marketing skills. Your favourite restaurant is La Galleria on Norton Street and your favourite bar is Tio's Tequila Bar in Surry Hills. You drink green tea, never coffee, and your cup size is thirty-two B.'

Brooke knew her mouth was open but she couldn't shut it. He was good. *Very* good. But clearly he didn't know everything. Although he did know her cup size? *Really?* How had he found that out?

'The internet does *not* give out information on cup sizes.'

'No…' Jack's eyes moved to her chest. 'That one I figured out by myself.'

Heat. More heat. Spreading across her chest and up her neck. She suddenly wondered if he liked small breasts.

What was she thinking? Jack Douglas would like *all* breasts.

'Fine. You know all my secrets. Time to tell me yours—why am I here, Jack?'

The waitress arrived back with her drink and made a show of setting up a napkin and making sure the straw was facing the right way. She was taking an awfully long time.

'Thank you.' Brooke looked up into two very large breasts. Definitely not thirty-two B. The waitress was leaning forward, her eyes fixed on Jack. Brooke turned to see Jack smile back at her. Right. Sleazebag. *So* not her type. She needed to get this over with.

When the waitress finally moved away, swaying her hips ridiculously as she walked, Brooke spoke. 'When you're finished lining up your next conquest, I'd like to know what you want from me.'

'You're a pushy little thing, aren't you?'

She hated being called little even more than she hated being called pushy. Even though she knew she was. But it was condescending and rude, and coming from Jack after the way he'd just ogled their waitress it made her even angrier.

'Yes, I'm pushy. Because I'm suspicious. I'm suspicious about why I'm here and what your motives are. But don't worry, Jack, it's not you. I'm pushy and suspicious with everyone.'

She'd always been that way. Sometimes she wished she was more trusting and easygoing, like her little sister Melody. She wished she could put on rose-coloured glasses and expect people to treat her with respect and be gentle. But people weren't like that. They were selfish. And most of the time they were too concerned with what was happening in their own little bubble to worry about hurting the feelings of those around them.

Jack smiled slowly. He leaned back, putting the heel of his shoe up to his knee. His muscles bulged. Brooke looked away. Muscles meant nothing to her. She spent hours in the gym with muscle-heads, and most of them had less between their ears than she had numbers in her little black book. Although she wasn't sure Jack was one of those guys who spent the hours they worked out taking selfies of their muscles. Jack seemed a little more worldly—a little more aware. Which made him infinitely more dangerous.

'That's interesting. Tell me more.'

Brooke smiled. 'Why would you think I'd tell you anything?'

'Because you're alone and you miss your sisters. Because you're feeling abandoned and you're angry and you need someone to talk to.'

Brooke opened her mouth to deny it but she couldn't. He knew exactly how she felt. How did he do that?

'Maybe I should be more like you and talk to no one about anything? Totally independent. An island.'

Jack's eyes hardened. 'No man is an island—haven't you heard?'

'*You* are.'

'That's where you're wrong, Brooke.'

Something in his tone stilled her. Something was different. *He* was different. As if he wanted to say something he wasn't saying. As if he wanted her to know something but couldn't tell her.

'Why can't you stand being touched?'

'What?'

'It's fairly obvious. Your eyes get all shifty whenever someone gets too close to you. You cross your arms and step back, and if anyone touches you I can practically see the hairs on your arms stand on end.'

Jack shifted, moving his leg back down. He moved forward, then back, before reaching for his drink again. When he'd sculled the last of it he motioned to the waitress. 'We're going to need a bottle of tequila, some lemon and some salt. And beers. Lots of beers.'

'I'm not drinking.'

'Yes, you are. You and I are getting ridiculously drunk tonight.'

'Why?'

'Because, Brooke, you make me uncomfortable. And the only way I can tell you what I want to tell you is if my brain is swimming in tequila.'

That statement sounded almost honest and it took Brooke aback a little that he'd admitted a vulnerability. A weakness. It seemed so off for Mr Cool to admit he was uncomfortable. Which was probably why she threw back two shots with him as soon as the tequila arrived a few minutes later.

After a long sip of beer Jack shifted back and Brooke shifted with him, resting her head on the cool leather cushioning of the bench seat. She turned her head to watch the side of his face.

'So are you going to tell me why I'm here? What you want from me?'

'I know why you're here, Brooke. I know you're trying to promote your family business.'

'So you mentioned.'

'Every person on this show has an agenda. Most are fame junkies, some are attention–seekers, and I suspect there are one or two who really are looking for love. But your motivation took me a little longer. Until that day on the beach and the red bikini. Which you looked unbelievably hot in, by the way.'

'I'm too skinny.'

'Your body is perfect. Strong. Healthy. Athletic.'

'I have no boobs.'

Jack turned to look at her breasts. He stared at them. Brooke felt heat rise up her throat as he studied her chest. His head moved and his eyes narrowed. Then—to her surprise—he lifted a finger and used it to pull her shirt aside. She slapped his hand away and shot him a horrified, disgusted look which he held. Steady. Her eyes against his.

No words were spoken but a conversation went on regardless.

How dare you touch me without permission?

You wanted an honest opinion on your breasts. I have to see them to give you one.

But I don't even know you and I definitely don't trust you. It's weird.

It's not weird.

Don't touch my skin.

I won't.

Don't check me out…sexually.

I will. But I won't touch your skin.

Brooke sighed, which meant, *Do it.*

So he did it, and even though he didn't touch her skin every cell on her body throbbed. Small bumps formed on her skin as the fabric slid away from her body. She felt the heat of his finger as it slowly traced her shirt, opening it wider so he could look inside. She watched his eyes—they were so close now. Dark and mysteriously unreadable. Then his lips parted slightly and her core throbbed even harder.

She wished he'd touch her skin. Accidentally. His

closeness reminded her of how long it had been since she'd been with someone. Since Mitch. Almost twelve months. Twelve months since a man's hands had made their way over her skin. Twelve months since she'd felt a man's lips on the back of her neck. Too long.

Jack's bottom lip stuck out and he moved his head from side to side before letting his finger drop from her shirt. But he didn't say anything.

'What's that supposed to mean?' she asked, anxiety bubbling in her chest. What the hell did that movement mean? Did he not like her breasts? What was wrong with them?

'Eh…' He shrugged and poured another two shots before settling back onto the leather seat to throw one back.

'Eh? *Eh?* That's what you have to say about my breasts? Eh? What the hell does *eh* mean?' He thought her breasts were *eh*? They were small, yes. But they were better than *eh*. Pig. Sexist pig. Knuckle-dragging, Neanderthal pig.

Brooke grabbed a shot and flung it back, enjoying the burn as it flew down her throat and into her stomach. Her head shifted. She hadn't been drinking much lately as she'd been focussing on training and the booze was going to her head. *Good.* She'd be able to say what she was thinking.

'Want to know what I think about *you*?' She was leaning forward now—too close for him to be comfortable, she knew, but she didn't care. Indignation burned at her temples.

'Not really, Brooke. You see—I'm not like you. I don't need people. I don't need their approval and I don't need anyone to like me.'

'Clearly. Is there actually anyone that you treat well?

Do you have any friends? What about your family? Are you as mean to them as you are to me?'

'I'm not mean to you, Brooke, I'm honest. There's a difference.'

'Yeah, there's a difference. It's called tact. If you were being honest you'd have some. Without tact you're just mean.'

Brooke was angry. Somehow this man always made her angry. Which was why the fact that she found him physically attractive was so annoying. And right now the way he was leaning back, all relaxed and comfortable, his dark hair sitting perfectly and a layer of stubble swathed across his jaw, he looked even more attractive than he ever had.

Brooke reached for the tequila bottle and poured two more shots. 'How about I employ your brand of tactless honesty? See how you like it?'

'Go ahead.'

He turned to smile at her and Brooke wondered how the hell he could look so boyishly gorgeous at the same time as looking like sex on a stick. It truly was a gift.

'I think you're lonely. I think you have Daddy issues. I think you have no friends because you have no idea how to treat people. I think you're mean and you're bad and you use your looks and your money to make friends and bed women. You're a bad person, Jack Douglas. Bad and mean.'

Brooke sucked back her tequila, not taking her eyes off him.

There was a pause before Jack lifted his head, held her eyes and spoke—in that deep, calm voice of his. '"Bed women"? Do people actually *say* that?'

'What? Yes. They do. Bed women. That's what you do.'

'Pretty sure I have sex with them. Sometimes I kiss them too.'

He smiled and Brooke felt it all across her body. The way he said sex. The way his eyes held her steady when he talked. The way his smile said *good boy* and his eyes said *badass sex god*. Brooke knew her breath was becoming shallower. She could hear herself breathing heavily and she wanted to stop it but she couldn't.

Slowly he reached for the bottle and topped up her shot glass before topping up his own. Then he drank and so did Brooke.

He placed his glass on the table and leaned in closer, his voice now dark and dangerous and way too deep to be legal. 'Sometimes I go down on them—and if they're very bad I might even spank them. *Bed* them hardly seems to say enough, does it?'

'No.' Brooke heard her voice squeak a little. 'It doesn't.'

Brooke leaned back. Away from his voice and his eyes and his provocative scent and those hands and those arms and his muscles and tattoos and everything else that was making the tequila rush to her head much too fast. No, no, *no*. Not this man. No.

'Jack.' There was a slight wobble to her voice so Brooke sucked in a breath. 'Why am I here?'

Thankfully Jack leaned back, too. But not before pouring another tequila and handing it to her. Brooke paused. Getting drunk was not a good idea. Not when thoughts such as what those vastus lateralis muscles looked like in the flesh kept pushing into her mind. She put the glass down and picked up her mineral water. She was here for business, not pleasure. He wanted something from her. Maybe if she gave it to him she could get the publicity she needed. But how much was that going to cost her? she wondered.

The pause after she spoke seemed to last a very long time. Jack looked down at his drink, then back up, then at her.

'I like you.'

'You *like* me?' Brooke was confused. What was he saying? The tequila was making her a little dizzy. 'What do you mean?'

'What do you think I mean?'

He looked away and stared into his drink again. What *did* he mean?

'I don't understand?' She felt anxiety coiled, poised. Ready to strike when he delivered his blow.

'I mean I like you. I like how you tell me things I don't want to hear. I like that you argue with me and fight with me and stop me from turning into...well, stop me from making bad choices. I want you and I to be...friends.'

He liked her. He wanted to be friends. Her friend. Not her lover?

She didn't want to be his friend. She wanted to kiss him and sleep with him and have him go down on her and spank her and all those other bad things he said he did. She didn't want to be friends. She wanted more and he didn't.

His rejection hurt. Just as Mitch's had hurt twelve months ago. Just as it had hurt when her parents had rejected her. It hurt and he wasn't getting away with it. Not this time. This time she was going to take it.

'No.'

'What?' Jack turned to her, clearly surprised.

'I said no.'

'No? No, I don't like you?' Now *he* looked confused,

as if he'd never heard the word *no*, let alone had anyone say it to him.

'No. You *do* like me. And I like you. But I don't want to be friends.'

'You don't?' He still looked confused as he turned the glass around in his hand. 'You don't want to be friends?'

'Stop saying that word.'

'What word? Friend?'

'Yes. *Friend*. I'm not your friend. Nor will I ever be your friend. I have enough friends. Real friends. Friends I actually like. I don't need any more friends.'

The silence that followed dragged out for what seemed like hours. Jack spun the glass in his hand. His right leg shook as he tapped his foot on the ground.

'Right. OK…' was all he said.

The silence stretched out for too many minutes. Jack didn't speak and neither did Brooke. But she didn't want to leave either.

'We need more tequila.'

Jack's eyes hit hers hard. She took him in—his dark eyes, the stubble on his jaw, his full lips. Her eyes trailed down his chest to the dark hairs that whispered at his neckline. She wanted him. She wanted to put her hands on him and her lips on him. She wanted him to feel something for her. She wanted him to stay.

Jack breathed in, long and hard. She waited for him to refuse her, for him to get up and leave. But he didn't.

'Hit me.'

CHAPTER EIGHT

THE TEQUILA WENT down fast. As it did so Brooke found her shoulders relaxing. She also found herself moving closer to Jack. Drunk Jack was a lot more entertaining that sober Jack. When he smiled at her Brooke noticed the crinkles at his eyes. Sexy. He was *so* sexy when he smiled.

'Tell me about you, Brooke. What were you like as a teenager? Wait—let me guess? Straighty-one-eighty, Miss Goody Two-Shoes, I-didn't-lose-my-virginity-until-I-was-eighteen?'

Brooke tried to be indignant but it was true. 'Nineteen, actually, and, yes, I was a good girl. Still am.'

'Good girls make the best bad girls,' he teased, his arm resting close to her shoulder but still not touching. Never touching.

Brooke felt her body heat. Mitch had never made her stomach flip and the heat curl low in her belly the way Jack did. 'Good girls make terrible bad girls. We think too much.'

'That's what makes you so good at being bad. You know what you're doing. When you decide to let yourself go you do it completely and without any hesitation. Confidence and knowing what you want is incredibly sexy.'

Brooke knew where this conversation was headed.

She really should stop it but the tequila said no. 'Sounds like you've had plenty of experience.'

'I have. But that's not a bad thing. It means you don't have to worry when you're with me. I'd satisfy you. I wouldn't give up until I did.'

'Ha! You wish.'

'I do wish, Brooke. I *do* wish.'

It was the sincerity in his tone that did it. It was the way he seemed really to mean what he said. Her brain knew that he didn't, but her stupid, needy, desperate tequila-laced heart wanted to believe he did.

Which was why she leaned in. Which was why she stared at his lips. And which was why, when the hotness of his lips met hers, she let herself go. Completely.

Jack pulled her bottom lip in between his teeth. This was what he'd been wanting to feel all night. Her. Close to him. So close he could taste her. And right now she tasted like lemon and salt and warmth and comfort and it was just what he needed. Especially after his terrific failure at actually trying to be honest with her earlier.

He'd struggled in the past few days. He'd thought about her so much. About the way she exposed his faults. The way she made him want to be better. He realised now it wasn't just lust. He liked her. Who she was. He wanted to let her in.

And then she'd arrived in her sexy shirt, almost open to the waist, and she hadn't let him get away with any-thing. She'd made him accountable, and she'd made him want to actually *talk*. She'd told him what she thought of him. That was unusual. People usually told him what he wanted to hear. He was surrounded by people too scared to annoy him, but she seemed to have no problem with it. Which was why he wanted more with her. But she'd refused. She'd said she had enough friends. *Real* friends.

But now she was moving her soft lips against his and exploring his mouth with her tongue—and it felt very friendly. And he wanted her close. Her hands snaked up his chest. He grabbed her wrists and held them back. She leaned against him, trying to press her skin to his, but he held her away. Her mouth he wanted close, but not her skin.

'Jack, what's wrong?'

'Nothing,' he murmured as his kisses moved from her mouth and down her neck.

She made a little mewling noise in the back of her throat and he knew he'd found her spot. It was at the base of her neck, and as she arched her back he kissed it again, letting his tongue flick the spot and his teeth tease her skin before soothing it with a hard kiss. She said she didn't want to be friends. He wanted more. Not just sex. *More.* But she didn't want that. He had to hold back. He couldn't fall. He couldn't get too close. He needed to protect himself.

'Jack…let me touch you,' she whispered as she pushed against his hands.

He had them held still. No, she couldn't touch him.

'Relax. Let me touch you.'

When he felt her wrists stop fighting against his hold he lifted a hand to cup her jaw and moved his mouth back to hers. Taking her lips, kissing her deeply, allowing her bad girl every excuse to escape. She was proving to be a wonderful bad girl. Responsive. Passionate. The noises she was making were making him even harder. The way she tried to push herself into him made his body heat and his brain blur. But not enough to stop him keeping her wrists held so she knew not to touch.

Slowly, carefully, he let his hand explore her skin. Down her jaw and neck and further down still, till he hit the soft mounds of her breasts. They *were* small, but perfect, and when he'd pulled her shirt away earlier he'd glimpsed a flash of dark pink. He wanted to feel her nipple now. Twist it between his fingers before licking at its hardness.

He moved his head and she seemed to encourage him as he kissed down her chest, but a loud cough to his right brought him back to reality. They were still in the bar. There were people either side of him. Public displays of affection were not his thing. He hadn't kissed a girl in a bar in years—too many camera phones had stopped that habit. But the combination of Brooke and tequila was making him do some very stupid things.

Like trying to get her naked right here in front of everyone. Like sleeping with a contestant. Like wanting more from her. That was a monumental mistake. Even through the tequila he knew that was wrong.

Quickly and efficiently he pulled her shirt back to where it was supposed to be and sat up. Brooke's eyes opened wide, as if she were coming out of a daze, and she rubbed the back of her hand across her mouth.

What the hell was he thinking? He'd become too carried away. She was so easy to talk to and she laughed in all the right places. It was as if he'd reverted back to his sixteen-year-old self for a second. Thinking that this girl was different. Thinking he could actually trust her. Of course he couldn't. The only reason she was here was to get publicity for her business, and the only reason she'd agreed to meet him tonight was because he'd forced her. Bullied her into getting what he wanted.

No, that wasn't him. He wasn't going to be like his father and make people do what he wanted even when they didn't want to. If she was going to be with him it would be because she wanted to. He had to pull back.

'Wow. I think we got a bit carried away.' A shy smile spread across Brooke's face and she lifted her eyes to his.

Jack's body tensed when he looked at her. Her hair was loose and curling round her shoulders, her lips dark red and her green eyes glowing in the low light. He wanted her even more than ever but he couldn't do anything about it. He had to stop. He could easily throw himself at her in here, but he wasn't going to do that. He liked her too much and that meant it would cut him too much when she left.

'We did. My mistake.'

No more tequila, Jack decided. Time for a real drink. He picked up the discarded Scotch on the table and took a sip. He hated the taste. He hated the burn. And he hated the way it reminded him of his father. Wouldn't his father celebrate if he could see him now? *Another mistake, Jacko? I knew you'd slip up.*

Jack sipped again—before almost spitting it out when he felt Brooke's hand on his thigh.

'What if it wasn't a mistake? What if it's what we both need?'

Jack felt his chest rise and fall. Something about Brooke made him uncomfortable. Not in a bad way but a confrontational way. She made him feel things he didn't want to and think things he wished he didn't have to. But he'd been handling it fine because she always delivered her messages with spit and fire. Now she was touching him, and her smile had gone sexy, and her lashes blinked. His eyes slipped to her breasts again. He wanted to touch them. He wanted to feel her body beneath him. And she wanted him—that was clear. But maybe it was just the tequila talking.

'What I need to do is take you home.'

Brooke's mouth drooped a little at the edges and he didn't like it that he'd done that. He liked it when he made her laugh. She had a wide smile and deep dimples, and when she flashed her white teeth she looked carefree and fun and everything he wished he could be.

'What's the matter? Are you scared?'

'Not scared. Sensible. You're a contestant. It's unethical.'

'What do you care about ethics?'

She had a point. 'I don't like messy.'

'Messy?'

Her eyebrows shot down and her hand moved away. Strangely, he missed it.

'It wasn't "messy" when you wanted to be friends—why would this be messy?'

'Because one of us would want more.'

Her smile was back. Wide and gorgeous.

'More? From you? I know better than to expect anything more from *you*.'

There it was. The reason she didn't want more. He wasn't good enough for her. Well, maybe he wasn't. But she didn't know that. She assumed she knew him. Had read about him in the papers, heard the rumours. But she didn't know him. She thought he just wanted sex. Well, he might as well live up to his reputation—she was determined not to like him anyway.

'Well, seeing as you expect the worst—let's go.'

She stared at him but didn't move. Just as he'd suspected. She hadn't meant what she'd said. She didn't want anything from him. He'd had enough. He wanted to go to bed. The tequila had given him a headache and with a staff meeting scheduled for tomorrow he was in for a big

day. This woman was doing his head in. She was complicated and confusing and he wasn't in the mood any more.

'OK.'

It was so quiet he thought he'd misheard, but then she
repeated herself.

'OK. Let's go.'

At those three words, Jack's whole body fired up.
She'd said OK. She wanted to go home with him. The
woman he wanted actually wanted him. But he shouldn't.
She was a contestant and she was fiery and she could
make trouble. *Sensible.* That was what he had to be.

But her hand was back on his thigh and she massaged
the muscle just above his knee. Then he watched as her
hand slid up his leg, closer and closer to his groin. Her
pink-painted nails glowed against the lighting in the bar.
He couldn't believe he wasn't throwing her hand off. He
didn't want her to touch him. He never wanted anyone
to touch him. But her hand was firm and confident—as
if she knew what she wanted. Good girl gone bad. They
were hard to find, but when you found one...

Brooke's hand expertly cupped him and he felt as if
he was going to explode. He wanted to stop what she was
doing but her hand moved again, up past his buckle and
over his chest. As if she was feeling every inch of him.
He didn't want her hands all over him but he couldn't stop
her. He was mesmerised by her fingernails.

When her hands hit the skin of his neck he finally
looked into her eyes. He saw lust and something else.
Something deeper. She lowered her chin and her mouth
was close again. He wanted to throw her back and kiss
her. He wanted to have his hands all over her. But he
held steady. He still couldn't figure out why he felt so
much for her. It was almost chemical—like a magnet attracted to iron. He couldn't stop thinking about her and

his mind refused to let him forget about her. Even though the logical part of his mind knew he shouldn't like her—the rest of him didn't care. He liked her. He wanted her. He had to have her.

Slowly, seductively, she leaned forward, and he felt her words on his ear before he heard them.

'Take me home, Jack, and make love to me.'

Jack didn't care if she was playing games. He wanted her and tonight she wanted him. He leaned in, catching a glimpse of her breasts, and touched his cheek to hers, wanting to feel her skin on his but needing to tell her what she needed to know. Needing to warn her.

'I want you *bad.*'

CHAPTER NINE

BROOKE LOST IT. She dropped her glass and it clattered onto the hardwood floor. She felt the breaths in her chest come way too fast. She needed air. She needed to breathe. But most of all she needed Jack Douglas. Tonight.

She didn't care what he meant about being friends. She didn't care that he was the producer. And she didn't care that soon she was supposed to meet her 'perfect match'. All she cared about was her skin being right next to his skin and his tongue sucking on her '*eh*' breasts.

'We need to leave.'

She didn't want to wait for the tequila to wear off or for herself to change her mind. Jack was bad and mean and no good. Perfect for one night of hot sex—which was exactly what she needed. No wonder she'd been so angry lately. Sex. That would fix it. After she had hot, hot sex with this very bad man she'd go back to being her normal, calm, sweet self. She could finish this stupid show and get the hell out of here.

'Leave?'

'Right now. We need to go.'

Brooke stood. If she didn't take him home right now the waitress would, and tonight *she* wanted him. She wanted to have sex with someone who knew what the hell they were doing. It had been too long. She'd been good for too long. Her sisters were right, she needed to do something mental to bust her out of the rut she was in. And Jack Douglas was certainly mental.

'Now.'

She didn't touch him but she gave him a look that she hoped left him in no doubt of her intentions. And if he was as bad as she suspected, and—let's face it—she knew he was, he'd follow her. He'd take her home and give her a seeing-to until she couldn't stand straight. Which was just what she needed, she'd decided. Or maybe the tequila had decided for her. Either way—it was happening.

Brooke walked out through the door with only a sliver of doubt that he'd follow. The doubt disappeared as soon as she felt the warm breeze hit her outside. She felt him behind her, heard his footsteps on the cobbles.

'Where are we going?'

Brooke turned, stopping but not touching him. 'Your place, obviously. There are eleven other women at my place.'

He smiled but didn't say anything. He didn't have to. She knew what he was thinking.

'I'm sure twelve women at once is a mild night for you, but tonight I want you all to myself. Just you and me—and you know what?'

'What's that, Brooke?'

She didn't miss the satisfaction in his voice.

'You're going to enjoy it. And you're going to make me enjoy it. You're going to pull out every trick you have in that bag of yours because I haven't had sex in twelve months and I need unbelievable sex tonight. Not good. Not even great. Un-freaking-believable. And, Jack? We're not friends. Can you do that?'

'I can try.'

'There's no *try*.'

Brooke turned to walk again. She wasn't sure where he lived, or where he was staying, but she wasn't about to stop and ask because if she did she might change her mind. She might think about tomorrow and how awkward it would be. She might also think about how she would probably enjoy it and might want to do it again, but he wouldn't, and then she'd get mad and offended and probably say something to him, and then he'd think she liked him and she'd try and explain that she didn't, and then he'd think she *really* liked him, and then she'd get really angry and start thinking about it and obsessing, and then she'd probably convince herself she actually wanted to see him again, and then he'd break her heart. *Sigh.*

Brooke stopped. This was going to end in tears, wasn't it?

'Something wrong?'

He was so close behind her but still not touching her. She wished he would touch her. Something to encourage her. Something to stop her from thinking and to remind her that this was about a bad boy and a night of fun.

Brooke breathed in a big gulp of muggy sea air. The tequila swam in her head. It was telling her things. Telling her to say things she didn't want to. But the tequila was strong.

'I haven't had a boyfriend in almost a year.'

Don't say that!

'Then you're well overdue for some attention.'

'My boyfriend left me.'

No! Not sexy.

'Your ex sounds like a jerk.'

'He's not. He wasn't. He was perfectly lovely and we were perfectly happy. One day he just didn't call. And he didn't answer my calls. And he was never home, and I couldn't get hold of him, and his friends kept feeding me excuses. I didn't know what the hell was going on until I saw a Facebook post a few weeks later. It was a picture of him and "his love". That's what he called her.'

Brooke didn't cry. She'd shed so many tears over Mitch that there were none left, but somewhere deep in her heart something twisted.

'He left me. Then he got someone else and posted it all over social media. Didn't even have the balls to tell me. Couldn't even give me a heads-up. Just humiliated me.'

Jack was silent behind her and she knew what he was thinking. She'd said too much. He didn't want to know. He didn't want heavy. He was a bad boy—he wanted light, fluffy bimbo. Not feelings. Bad boys didn't *do* feelings.

Bloody tequila!

Brooke started to walk before she thought about what she'd said and before he could say anything to her. She'd blown it. There'd be no hot sex with Jack tonight. She'd been humiliated by a man in the past—why the hell would she want to do something that was sure to lead to more humiliation?

Brooke's feet started to move faster and so did her anger. It escalated as she remembered every sexist, horrible thing Jack Douglas had done to her. It escalated when she thought of the girls back at the penthouse. All believing they were going to find their perfect match on the show. All believing that there was a man out there who was going to make them happy.

It seemed only she knew the truth. Men didn't make you happy—they made you miserable. The only person you could count on was yourself.

Brooke's feet stopped and a massive lump caught fiercely in her throat. Then why had she been so miserable since Mitch left? Why had she let her happiness depend on him being around? Mitch. Who had left her for no reason. Who hadn't even said goodbye. Who hadn't even had the decency to tell her it was over to her face.

He'd left her a message. A very public, very humiliating Facebook message on her wall. Everyone had known he'd left her. *Breathe in, breathe out.* She'd been humiliated. Exposed. Which was exactly what she was going to feel in a few weeks, when this show aired. When the men arrived tomorrow and she failed all the challenges and didn't get to meet anyone. When it was her time to fail, like Alissa had at the beach. *Keep moving. Keep walking.* She started to walk again.

'Brooke. Stop.'

Jack's deep voice was close behind her. Only a few steps away. The sound of it made her move. Quickly. But his long legs against her short ones meant he was keeping up. So she walked faster and faster, until both her feet were off the ground and she was jogging. But he was still keeping up.

'You can't outrun me, you know.'

Challenge accepted.

Brooke paused to slip off her heels and broke into a run. An all-out pelt up the Corso and across the road to the beach. The sand would slow him down. But it didn't. Once she reached the bottom of the stairs and her heels started to dig into the sand he was right beside her, arms pumping.

'Faster Brooke, faster!' She heard her father's voice ringing in her head.

She ran faster. Faster and faster towards the water. Wanting to get away. Wanting to forget. Wanting not to think, just to breathe and pump her legs.

When her feet hit the water it was cold and she braced herself as she dived in. She dipped her head, allowing the noises of the ocean to take all her thoughts and worries and anxieties and humiliations away. She swam and stood and dived and swam until her lungs burned. Then she stopped. She was a long way out. Past the breaking waves. The water was black and everything around her was black. She was alone, and the exhilaration she'd been feeling as she swam was quickly replaced with fear.

When Jack's arms grabbed her from behind her first feeling was an irrational terror that it was a shark. When she turned and looked at his face she realised he was a shark. He was beautiful. Wet and dripping, his face shadowed, his eyes hooded. He had his shirt off and he was panting and his eyes were fixed on her lips.

'I know you're angry, Brooke.'

His voice was low and deep and Brooke felt it rumble through her chest.

'I can make you feel better.'

Jack Douglas was a bad man. A man who partied hard, broke hearts and didn't care about anyone or anything. He *was* a shark.

'I want to make you feel better.'

Right now he was telling her exactly what she wanted to hear. He knew what he was doing. *She* knew what he was doing. But for some reason she couldn't stop pressing her lips to his and kissing him as if it was her last day on earth.

Brooke's body felt as good as it looked. Her skin was smooth where his hands explored her wet flesh. Jack pushed the fabric of her shirt out of the way so he could come into contact with her skin. His aversion to touching was forgotten as his other hand came up to cup her chin. She was beautiful—but here in the ocean, all wet and frantic, she was out of this world.

Her eyes closed as he let his mouth press to her lips. He pushed in hard and she met him. Her kisses weren't soft or tender, and her passion was turning him on. She wanted him badly and he felt exactly the same. Their tongues explored and her hands were moving as wildly as her lips, touching everywhere. He didn't mind. He wanted her close.

He pushed and she pushed, and while his legs paddled wildly to keep them afloat he pressed closer, making sure they were as close as two people could be. He wanted her close. He wanted to hold her up and keep her afloat. He wanted to take her anger away, make her forget.

Brooke wrapped her legs around his waist. She clearly wanted to get closer to him, and her desire was unexpected and all the more sweet because of it. He suspected that right now she was hurting and wanted to hurt him as well. She wanted to make him feel how angry she was.

Her teeth bit at his lip and he growled a little. He tasted the salt on her skin as he kissed past her lips to her ear, then down the milky column of her neck. She threw her head back and moaned wildly as his kisses made their way down her chest.

He needed more traction. He wanted to do more with this beautiful mermaid. He wanted to lay her in the sand and kiss her all over. He wanted to take her anger until she wasn't angry any more—just wild with passion. For him. And only him.

Jack pulled back quickly. What was he doing? She wouldn't want to be with him. Not when she met her perfect match. Not when she realised he wasn't good at communication and feelings and all the other things that went on in relationships.

'Don't stop.' Her voice was soft and demanding.

'We should go back to shore.'

'No!'

Her legs tightened around his waist, making his erection painfully hard.

'I want to stay here. With you.'

She kissed him again and he felt as if he were drowning in it. Every thought and reason flew from his head. All he could concentrate on was the way his heart was beating faster and how he wanted to get close, closer to her and her skin, and her mouth and her hands. Her small body clung to him and he wrapped his arms around her, holding her close, wanting this to be something that it wasn't. He knew what this was. A fleeting moment of lust. He had to stop it before he got in too deep.

Pulling her arms from around his neck, he met her eyes. 'Brooke, we have to go back.'

She understood. He saw her eyes searching his. She was thinking, but he didn't know what.

When she let him go he felt cold and bare and he hated that he felt it. This was why you couldn't get close. The confusion and the wondering what the other person was thinking. He'd not had a relationship yet that was honest and he was sure it would be the same with Brooke. She confused the hell out of him already, with her arguing and fighting and then her unexpected kisses.

He watched as she took skilful strokes through the water to the shore. He wasn't a strong swimmer. He hoped she didn't turn around when she reached the sand to watch him. She was athletic—good at everything. He wondered how she did that. And she was smart and hot. She was stunning and special.

But not *his* special, he reminded himself as his feet finally hit the sand and he was able to stand and step over the gently rolling waves to the shore. His breathing was heavy. He hadn't been to the gym in three months. Ever since work on this show had started.

He missed it. He missed seeing his workout on the board and thinking there was no way he'd complete it in time, then the satisfaction when he did. He felt unfit right now, and he was sure Brooke would want someone fit. She was so fit herself. Women like her put value on health and fitness and he caught himself wishing he were fitter. Wishing he could impress her—because so far he hadn't been able to, and that was starting to bother him.

When he made it past the water she was waiting for him. Soaking wet. Her hair was pulled back and her face was shining in the moonlight. He'd never wanted to kiss anyone more, but he didn't. He couldn't. This would never work. She'd get hurt, and something deep inside him knew he didn't want to hurt her.

But she didn't give up that easily. She stepped forward, wrapped her arms around his waist and leaned her head on his chest. That was all. Just quietly stood there, hugging him tight. It was an intimate feeling and he wanted to push her away. Explain that he didn't *do* intimate. But right then it seemed as if she needed him and he liked it. She needed comfort and warmth and understanding and he wanted to give it to her.

He let his arms envelop her. Maybe he couldn't give her a lifetime of happiness, but he could give her a moment. He could make her feel better for now. As his arms tightened she looked up. The smile she gave him was relaxed and grateful and he was so glad he'd done that. He liked to make her smile even more than he liked to fire her up. Which was why he leaned down to kiss her.

But the comforting kiss soon turned into something more. Her hands explored his chest, her tongue eager and exploring. He let his hands rest on either side of her face, keeping her still, keeping her there—not letting her go. Something wild and frantic built inside him. He wanted her. He needed her. He had to have her. Here. *Now.* Carefully and quickly he wrapped one arm behind her back and let her fall to the sand.

Brooke wasn't angry any more. The emotion she was feeling now was something else. Something much more desperate. She wasn't sure if it was still the tequila doing the thinking, but right now she felt something from Jack she hadn't felt in a long time. He wanted to please her. He wanted to comfort her. And she was grateful—because she was lonely and sad and angry and his comfort was exactly what she needed.

When he pushed her back into the sand Brooke felt strangely safe. He was strong and he was leading her to where she needed to be. She didn't have to think—all she had to do was feel.

'Are you sure you want to do this? With me?'

When she looked at him she was surprised at the uncertainty in his eyes. She'd never seen that look before. She hadn't ever considered he'd be insecure. Didn't he realise how much she wanted him?

'Yes. I want this. I want *you.*'

He didn't smile, but he held her eyes before kissing her. His soft lips soothed her and Brooke's head swam. She thought of nothing but him, and the weight of him on top of her, and the feeling of his hands running over her body.

Keeping one hand on her waist, with the other he pulled at her shirt. Moved the wet fabric aside, as well as the bra underneath, to expose her thirty-two B breasts. His tongue laved at her nipple and any residual anger in Brooke's head gave way to something else. A pleasure that made thinking impossible. That made reason vanish. She just wanted more. More of his mouth and more of his tongue and more of *him*.

The cool night air hit her nipples and they hardened. He took them in his mouth again before allowing his lips to trail further down her stomach. With a tug he managed to get her wet jeans off. He threw them in a heap on the sand and Brooke clawed at him, trying to get him back up to kiss her again. But he didn't. He stayed where he was.

'You're beautiful,' he murmured as his tongue licked around her lower stomach.

Brooke lay still in anticipation of his touch. Of his tongue. His kisses moved lower and she opened her legs, allowing his head to get closer. She watched him. Watched the way his eyes eagerly drank her in. She watched his hands as they stroked her thighs, and then she watched as he trailed one finger through her wetness.

'So wet... So hot...' he murmured, before allowing his face to fall and his tongue to push in, searching for her clit.

Brooke arched her back in delight. She moaned, grabbed at the sand, trying to get some traction—but there was none so she reached for his shoulders instead. Looking down, she watched him as ripples of pleasure shuddered through her. She pushed her pelvis up, wanting to get closer, needing him to go deeper, and he obliged. His tongue worked like magic and he sucked gently, making her groan even louder.

This was what she needed. Pure release. With a man who knew what he was doing. Mitch had never done this properly and he'd certainly never been this enthusiastic.

Jack's head moved a little from side to side and Brooke almost screamed. That slight movement had his tongue hitting every G-spot she had. She wanted more…she needed more. She was building fast.

'Don't stop,' she moaned, pushing herself closer and closer to him.

He didn't stop. His movements became more frantic. His tongue started to move in and out and up and down and then he made a low, growling noise that she felt reverberate through her whole body.

That did it.

The orgasm started down low but once it took hold Brooke couldn't stop it. It grew inside her like a werewolf howling at the moon till she felt it burn through her veins, up her stomach and into her arms. Her whole body shook and still he didn't stop. She felt him suck and the orgasm shot through her again, even more powerful than before.

'Stop, stop! You have to stop.'

She pushed on his shoulders, trying to get him to release her. She was swollen and sensitive and her brain felt as if it were about to burst.

With one last tender kiss, Jack moved. He looked up, his face flushed and his eyes glowing.

Brooke didn't move. She couldn't. Her body lay in satisfied pleasure.

'That was…that was…' She couldn't speak. She couldn't explain how good she felt.

Then she felt him next to her. His arms weren't on her, but he lay next to her. His skin was still wet but she was hot so it felt good.

Brooke lay panting for a few more minutes before she turned in the sand to look at him. He had one hand behind his head and was staring up to the moon, but he turned when she looked at him. A slow smile spread across his face.

'Feeling better?'

'Much better.'

Brooke shifted and spread an arm across his chest. She felt him immediately stiffen beneath her so she withdrew her arm. Even after what had happened he still didn't want her to touch him. She should have been offended, but she was too relaxed and relieved to feel anything but curiosity.

'Why don't you like being touched?'

'I do. I was enjoying you touching me earlier.'

He was smiling, but she wasn't fooled.

'That's different. You don't like anyone hugging you or putting their hands on you. You get nervous when I touch you. Like right now—you went stiff when I tried to cuddle you. And today, in the hospital, you hated that I was holding your hand.'

He was quiet and Brooke turned to face the moon, wondering if he'd answer.

'I don't like insincerity.'

'Touching is insincere?'

'It is when you hardly know someone. I just don't understand why you would want someone that close to you.'

'Because it feels good. Because everyone needs physical touch. Because people like to feel loved and cherished and they want people to show them.'

'I just don't like lies.'

That made Brooke turn. 'That's hilarious, coming from you.'

His eyes met hers. They were hard and challenging. 'I may be an emotionless, indifferent, unfeeling, apathetic bastard—but I'm not a liar.'

Brooke laughed. She couldn't help it. There clearly was no one who could abuse Jack better than he could himself. 'You're a bit hard on yourself, lover.'

Jack propped himself up on his hand and looked at her, his smile back. 'Lover? Is *that* what I am?'

'Yes. You are. If you think we're not going to do that again you're wrong. That was…you were…magnificent. And I *don't* think you're emotionless and indifferent and unfeeling and—what was the other thing?'

'Apathetic.'

'Right. Apathetic. I think you're passionate and thoughtful and you care more than you think you do.'

Jack didn't take his eyes off her. He watched her watching him and Brooke started to feel an uncomfortable feeling settle over her. As if she was thinking too much about him and wanting too much of him. But then she felt the warmth of his hand on her shoulder. Brooke held her breath as his hand slid down her arm to her waist, where it rested. She knew what this was. Jack's form of post-sex snuggling.

Brooke sucked her core in tight. She didn't know what it meant, but it made her nervous. Something was happening and she was very afraid it was another thing she wouldn't be able to control.

CHAPTER TEN

TODAY THE MEN were arriving. The tone of the show was about to change. Testosterone was about to be introduced, meaning more aggression, more competition and even more drama. Perfect. Just what the show needed.

Jack sat watching the reel Mick had edited so far. It had the lot. Dramatic scenes, backstabbing, lots of flesh and a few tears. His blood was running hot. He was sure this time he'd have a hit. He'd managed to find that perfect combination of personalities and format. This show would be a success and then he could get out. For good. Away from this lifestyle, away from these people and away from the rumours.

But Jack's shoulders were still tense and tight. This wasn't over yet. But—surprisingly—he wasn't worried. Far from it—he was excited. He was fired up. He kept shooting questions and suggestions at Mick. He wanted to watch the reels again and again. He felt buzzed, as if he'd spent the night drinking coffee. But he hadn't. He'd spent the night alone in his bed. Not sleeping, but being kept wide awake by the memory of two green eyes, a petite body and a pair of thirty-two B breasts.

Brooke Wright shouldn't be stuck in his head. But she was. The way she tasted when he kissed her salty skin. The way her frantic kisses made him feel bigger, stronger and needed. She was desperate for him, angry and crazy, and he shouldn't even be thinking twice about her, or that kiss, but it was stuck in his head. *She* was stuck in his head and he couldn't shake her. And somewhere in the night he'd had an epiphany.

'It's good, Jack, but…'

'But what?'

'The female audience are not going to like the men calling the shots.'

'No, they're not. Which is why we're switching it up. The women are going to determine the challenges.'

Mick didn't move. He was waiting.

'We've been concentrating too much on drama for getting our ratings, Mick, but we were wrong.'

'We were?' Mick asked quietly.

'We were. We need to focus on emotions. On relationships. We need the drama to come from the way the women *feel*. If we leave it up to the men this will all be about ridiculous and demeaning challenges. That's surface stuff. We're going to dig deeper—and who better to dig deeper and get to the core of something than a woman?'

Mick stayed silent.

'The women will determine the challenges—they'll make the men work for them. They'll force the men to talk and to feel and to try harder. That's good TV.'

Mick breathed in through his nose quickly, then released it slowly. 'It's risky, Jack. It's harder to capture emotion on tape. It's harder to edit. It'll take longer, and it'll cost more.'

'But it will make better TV and that's the point.'

Jack waited. If Mick didn't agree he wasn't sure what he'd do. He respected Mick. His opinion was like gold in this industry. He'd been around for ever, had seen everything. He knew what worked and what didn't. And Jack wanted this to work. Not just because he believed in it but because it was the right thing to do. He'd forgotten what TV shows were about as he searched for ratings and audiences and advertising dollars. Storytelling. Emotions. Human reactions. And that was what he needed to get back.

'Let's give it a go.'

Jack breathed out and slapped Mick on the back. Today was a good day.

Jack paced his office floor one more time. The sound of Brooke's heavy breathing in his ear rang through his brain. He thought of the feel of her skin under his hands, smooth and wet. His chest actually hurt, thinking about her. He was seventeen again and finding it very hard to control himself. He'd tried not to think about her, tried to distract himself as he sorted out the last of the male contestants and rewrote the format. But it wasn't working.

He found himself reaching for his car key, determined to drive over there and find out what she was thinking and if she'd changed her mind about being friends. But he stopped himself. She didn't want more. If she did she'd have contacted him. She'd have let him know. But she didn't. He had to get that through his thick head.

With the editing done it was time to get to the penthouse and start getting the girls ready for the big scene later on today. Meeting the men. And letting them know that *they*—the women—were now determining the challenges. He was looking forward to it, but more than that he was looking forward to seeing Brooke again. Which he knew he shouldn't be.

Ever since they'd met he'd known there was something between them. A little spark of sexual energy that he'd thought would go nowhere. She had seemed too up-tight to do anything like she had the other night. And the other night she had been anything but uptight. No—stop. He had to shake this off. He needed to go for a work-out, a run—or maybe go and have sex with a beautiful stranger. Anything to get Brooke and her green eyes out of his head.

But he didn't want to have sex with anyone else. He wanted to finish what he'd started with her.

He drove silently through the city and back over the bridge to Manly. The sun was out and burning even brighter today. A perfect Sydney Sunday. Jack hadn't felt this fired up in years. Today's shoot was a big one. The girls were spending most of the day in hair and make-up—getting styled for the big meet-and-greet this after-noon. The men were being bussed in at three. This scene was important. He needed to make sure there was enough sex in the air to make it spicy and enough tension to have everyone almost wetting themselves in anticipation.

He didn't usually get this involved in the day-to-day of any show. But this time he was determined to be there every step of the way. This time there would be no mis-takes like last time.

A flashback of the fight scene ran through his mind. If he had been there he would have stopped it from get-ting out of control. The scene had rated well, but the com-plaints afterwards had seen the show pulled off the air and millions go down the drain. His father hadn't been impressed. Jack had dreaded the call from his house in Italy.

'How the hell did you let that happen, Jack?'

Useless, stupid idiot…should have known better than to leave you in charge…

It had been his father at his worst.

The names and jibes hadn't bothered him. He'd already heard everything his father could possibly call him throughout his life. But the way he'd felt afterwards had. He'd been used. Manipulated. He'd assumed someone needed him and they hadn't. He should have known not to get so close. But he'd been younger then. Filled with ridiculous heroic tendencies. Now he was older and knew that getting too close always ended in disaster. You couldn't trust anyone.

He could see some of the girls up on the balcony as soon as he pulled up. He'd collected twelve of the most beautiful women in Australia for this show. Blonde, brunette, redhead—they were all gorgeous. But none was more stunning that the woman he was now trying to forget.

Brooke's chest hurt from the rapid beating of her heart and her dry throat itched. She checked the clock. Ten minutes till Jack Douglas arrived. Ten minutes till he walked through that door, all smiles and cockiness, and ten minutes till all her pride disappeared. Her entire insides felt as if they were going to come up out her throat.

Why the hell had she done that the other night? Why the hell had she let her emotions turn into something she really didn't want? Before, Jack Douglas had been a player, but she had had his number. She'd been driving the bus. But now she'd kissed him. She'd opened her legs for him and pushed her nipples wantonly into his mouth. Now *he* was driving the goddamn bus and she wanted to get off.

It had been three days since they'd had fun in the sand. He'd taken her home. Kissed her goodnight, then left. She'd waited to hear from him—sure he'd felt something. But clearly he hadn't. She hadn't seen him or heard from him and now she felt stupid. He'd been drunk on tequila that night. He hadn't really wanted to do that and he didn't want any more. He'd made no promises, but she'd assumed. She'd assumed he wanted as much as she did. And now here she was—disappointed and angry and feeling like a fool.

Breathe. Deep breaths. That was what she needed.

Around her nervous excitement was almost making a fog in the air. The other girls were sipping champagne and their voices were getting higher and higher. The men were arriving today. Their competition on the beach had been a warm-up. A prelude to the *real* competition. She suspected the producers—or Jack Douglas—had wanted the girls to bond and make friends before the men arrived. That way, when they started getting their hearts broken and getting rejected, their responses would be even more dramatic.

She knew what he wanted. A few 'That-Bitch-Stole-My-Man' moments. Great TV. But an awful, awful thing to create. Did the man have no shame? No. Of course not. He didn't even *know* her. He'd known she'd had too much to drink. He'd known she was angry and upset and he'd taken advantage of her. He had no morals. No idea of consequences. Just as she'd assumed, Jack Douglas was a take-whatever-he-wanted kind of guy.

And in ten…no, *eight* minutes he was going to walk through that door, throw her a knowing wink and shatter her confidence. Which was something she didn't really need. Not now the men were arriving. Twelve tall, handsome men. Twelve men and one perfect match. Twelve men she wouldn't even get a look-in with. Because she would only be able to go on dates with them if she won the challenges—and she never won anything.

If there was ever a time she'd needed to talk to her

sisters it was now. She needed Maddy to calm her down, Melissa to tell her she was awesome, and Melody to... Well, Melody would just ignore Brooke's problems and talk about her own. But that would be fine! At least Brooke wouldn't have to talk about her own problems then. She'd be distracted and she wouldn't keep checking the clock...

Seven minutes. She started to pace. She joined a small circle of three women in the lounge. She needed to find her Zen. Jack could throw whatever he wanted at her, but she was going to remain Zen. *Breathe.*

'I wonder if they'll be hot?' Katy looked at the other girls anxiously.

'Of course they'll be hot. They don't put *fuglies* on a show like this. Who wants to watch fuglies?' Alissa was back to her normal self and completely over her near-drowning experience.

'I don't care what they look like. I'm after a man with a good heart,' another girl said.

'What about you, Brooke? What are you hoping for?'

Brooke almost spat out her sip of water—she didn't trust herself around alcohol any more.

'What?'

'What are you hoping these men are like? What's your perfect match?'

Her perfect match? Jack's face swam in front of her eyes. His muscled body and those tattoos that skipped all the way down his arm to his wrist. She remembered how good it had felt when he'd finally let his palm run over her arm to her waist. Then, when it had travelled back up and his thumb had rested on her bottom lip, he had kissed her. Long and hard and deep.

Everything in Brooke's core suddenly went hot and heavy. He wasn't her perfect match. He was careless and thoughtless and he hadn't called in three days. She *hated* him.

Brooke shifted her eyes, aware of the cameras all around them. There were even more than normal here tonight. Set up right in their faces. Waiting for every word. Brooke smoothed down her skirt and shifted. She was wearing a Wright Sports watch tonight. She moved her hand, trying to get it into the shot. That was what she was here for, she reminded herself—not to meet her perfect match!

Everyone was waiting for her response. She checked her watch. Three minutes. What was she going to say? What would her sisters want her to say? What would be the best thing to say for the sake of the business? What could she say that wouldn't make her look like a fool in front of the man who was now making her armpits feel like the inside of a Swedish sauna?

'My perfect match is a nice cup of tea and a piece of chocolate cake.' She smiled.

The women laughed. Except for Katy.

'No, really, Brooke—what are you looking for?'

Brooke glanced at her. Katy *knew*. She knew Brooke was avoiding the subject. She wanted the truth.

Katy had been up when she'd got home the other night, and even though Brooke hadn't told her what had happened Katy had known something was wrong. She'd been asking her for days if she was OK.

'It was a joke, Katy.'

'You're so funny, Brooky,' said Alissa, giving her an embrace.

Katy didn't say any more. Brooke's shoulders relaxed. She still missed her sisters, but somehow these women had become her temporary family. She wasn't even as angry any more. The girls had begun to recognise when she was firing up and now they helped her calm down. Backed off. Gave her food. Told her a joke. She'd even started to enjoy herself.

Until she saw a camera and realised that none of it was real. Just as the other night hadn't been real. Nothing Jack had said or done had been real.

Except that orgasm.

Brooke folded her legs tighter as heat surged there. That had been real—and unbelievable—and the most stunning orgasm she'd ever had. And, although it annoyed her, she wished she could feel it again. But she knew she couldn't. That was over.

Brooke's thoughts were interrupted by a flurry of activity at the door. More cameras had arrived. Producers had started to make their way through the door and Brooke held her breath, waiting for her first glimpse of the man she'd decided she'd never wanted to see ever, ever again.

Jack's eyes scanned the room from outside the door. He looked at each of the faces of the twelve women assembled but saw none of them except the one face he couldn't get out of his mind. Brooke—like the rest of the women—looked angry and shocked.

Something about her look made his stomach drop. What had happened *now*? He wanted to go to her. He wanted to put his arms around her, make her laugh—take her anger away. But he couldn't Not here.

'Jack, we've got problems.'

Mick was at his side and his quiet voice sounded anxious. Mick was never anxious—which put Jack immediately on alert.

'What's happened?' Jack looked around. Some of the

women looked noticeably shaken. A couple were on the couch, comforting each other.

'Rob Gunn was here before you.'

'What?' Rob Gunn? His father's hotshot producer? What the hell had *he* been here for?

'The format is staying as it is, Jack. The men are determining the challenges. Rob announced it all to the girls—said they had to fight for their places. Told them to consider their friends their enemies and reminded them this is a competition. It wasn't good, Jack.'

Jack's blood burned red. His father had done this. His father had sent Rob here. He'd known it was a mistake to have told him about the revised format. He'd known he should have done this on his own.

'Where is he now?'

'Gone. But he showed me his contract, Jack. Signed by your father. It's legit. He's in charge now.'

Anger burned white-hot in Jack's ears. Not this time. Jack was in charge and his father wasn't calling the shots here. *He* was. He'd had enough—enough of playing his father's game, enough of putting up with his father's demands and enough of not getting angry. Tonight he was taking control of his life.

'Get him on the phone, Mick. This ends now.'

'This is ridiculous.'

When the door had opened and the stranger had appeared Brooke had known immediately that something was up. Where was Jack? Who was this new man? And when the perpetually happy man who'd said his name was Rob Gunn had announced that the men would be setting the challenges, and that there would only be four men, Brooke's anger had fired up again. It was bad enough she had to compete in challenges, but challenges chosen by four men who all seemed as if they shared half a brain between them was quite another thing.

'Since when do the men get to choose the challenges? The original format said we'd complete challenges set by the producers and we'd get to choose the men. What's going on?'

Rob Gunn had left now, but Mick had just come back into the room. He didn't appear to have much to say.

'Where's Jack? Does he know about this?'

'Look, ladies, I don't know what's going on right now. This was Jack's original idea but...'

This was *Jack's* idea? Of course it was. He was a sexist pig, she reminded herself. No matter how good he was at convincing her that he wasn't. No matter how talented he was with his tongue.

'This is embarrassing and demeaning. You can't make a major change like that without telling us.'

Mick stood. He rushed over to her and the cameras fell back.

'No, Mick!' Brooke's voice was getting louder. 'It's not right. Do you mean to tell me that now only four women will have the chance to meet their perfect match? That now we'll have to fight each other for the chance? This is silly.'

Mick was trying to calm her down, but she didn't want to be calmed down. This was outrageous.

'Calm down, there, love. All you girls have an equal chance of getting to meet us. There's no need to get your knickers in a knot—*you* might be one of the lucky ones.'

One of the four men Rob Gunn had introduced earlier spoke up.

Brooke turned slowly. She stared at him. 'My knickers are none of your business—*love*. And I can tell you right now I would be anything *but* lucky if I ended up with *you.*'

'Brooke, calm down. Jack will be here soon. I'll talk to him. We'll get this sorted. Just wait. Sit. Wait. I'll talk to Jack.'

'You'd better.'

She knew this wasn't Mick's fault, but her blood was boiling and her bones were shaking. She *wouldn't* fight the other women for these men. She *wouldn't* pit herself against women she'd become friends with. And if Jack thought he was going to make her he clearly didn't realise how angry she could get.

CHAPTER ELEVEN

JACK'S ANGER HAD subsided. A little. He'd managed to gain back a little control. He'd finally tracked down Rob Gunn, who was hiding in a luxury apartment owned by Jack's father. Jack had laid down the law. Told him to stay the hell away from the set *and* the girls.

Rob Gunn had reached for his phone, but Jack had reached for his as well. He'd done his research. He knew about the formal complaints of sexual harassment brought against Gunn in his last job. He knew Gunn wouldn't want that made public.

It had been enough to get rid of Gunn, but not his father. His father was adamant the format stayed the same, determined that the men would be calling the shots. Jack knew that was suicide. Women would hate it and they were the ones watching. It would turn them off. There'd be no chance of a spin-off. And, more important than that, it wasn't the right thing to do. Brooke had made him realise that.

The next person he wanted to see was his mother. He wanted to make sure his father didn't get to her first.

But he was too late. When he got to his mother's house her eyes were bloodshot and her normally perfect hair was in a mess.

'I yelled at him, Jacky...'

Jack remembered the way his mother's eyes had used to look. Soft and blue and wrinkled at the sides. Now she used Botox. It kept the wrinkles at bay. She didn't need it. He preferred the way she looked without it.

'It's all right, Mum, you don't have to worry about it. I have it under control.'

His mother had been pouring herself a drink and Jack jumped as he heard the glass smash against the wall. Quickly he went to his mother. It wasn't like her to lose her temper. His father must have really rattled her, Jack fumed. Right then he made his mind up to get on a plane to Italy and sort that man out once and for all.

'No, Jack, I *do* have to worry. I don't want you to fight for me. You're my son—not my protector. It's time I fought for myself.'

Jack stilled. His mother's voice was raised. She never raised her voice. She was always cool. Always calm.

'Mum, what's wrong? What did he say to you?'

'Nothing! Nothing more than what he usually says. It's not him that's making me angry now, Jack, it's *you*.'

'Me?' He'd done everything to try and fix this.

'Yes—you. When are you going to learn? When are you going to grow up? When are you going to realise that you can't control your father? He's the type of man who does whatever he wants.'

'I know who he is, Mum, but that doesn't mean he can treat you like he does.'

'Oh, Jack…' His mother poured the drink and fell into a nearby armchair. She lifted her arms, took her earrings out and placed them on the table next to her. 'Honey, sit down. It's time we talked.'

So Jack sat. And he listened.

'Your father is a passionate man. He throws himself headfirst into things. That's his charm. That's what I fell for. When we met he chased me. He pursued me and made me feel I was the only girl in the world. I felt like the most important person in the world. I thought that meant he loved me. But I was just something he wanted. After he had me the novelty wore off. He moved on. I could have left. I considered it. But you were so young and you loved him—he was so good to you then. He'd take you everywhere with him and lavish you with presents and attention.'

'And then he'd leave.'

'Yes, then he'd leave. But you have to realise that people don't always stay. People like your father have a full tank of love but they use it up quickly and madly. Then they need to leave and go and fill that tank again.'

'That just sounds like an excuse for him to do whatever the hell he wants.'

'I could have left, Jack, but what would have been the point? I loved your father. I wanted him so badly I was willing to put up with him going elsewhere because I knew he'd come back. He always came back.'

'You *knew*?' Jack felt the blood drain from his face.

He reached for his mother's hand but she pulled it away. His mother didn't like touching either.

'Of course I knew, Jacky.'

She knew. He'd been trying to protect her, but she knew. And she didn't look sad—just exhausted.

'I should have ended it years ago. I should have been more angry. I should have yelled and screamed and demanded he stay with me. But I didn't. I shut up and I put up.'

Jack finally really saw his mother. For the first time. Not as someone who needed his protection, but someone who needed his love. His mother had lived for thirty years with little affection. Always feeling second-best. He saw how lonely she was. She was right: she should have got angry years ago. Just as he was angry now.

'Never again.' When she looked at him determination lit his mother's eyes. 'Your father will be back—when this affair is over—but this time I won't be there. I'm tired, Jack, and I'm lonely. I need to find someone who cares about me. I need to be happy and it's taken getting angry for me to be able to do that.'

'Do you love him?'

'Do I *love* him? I have no idea—I'm not sure I even know what love is any more. Or if I'll ever meet anyone I love as much as your father. But the truth is all you can really hope is that you'll meet people to spend a few moments of your life with. Share some good times. Make some wonderful memories. I don't know if I'll love again, Jack, but it doesn't matter because I have you. I love you, and you love me, and our love is stronger and more real than any love I'll ever have with a lover.'

Jack stared out of the window as he approached the bridge. He'd spent so many years worrying about his mother, thinking she needed his protection. But that wasn't what she needed. She just needed *him*. Being there and making her laugh when she needed it. Letting her know that she was loved when she'd spent so much time feeling unloved.

He wished his mother had got angry years ago. He wished she'd realised years ago that his father was never coming back. But she was angry now and Jack was pleased for it.

The girls looked nervous when he arrived for the challenge. They were being kitted out in climbing suits and ropes. He wasn't sure if Brooke looked nervous or not because he didn't want to look at her. He remembered the sadness in his mother's eyes. Loving someone who didn't love you back was pointless. He wasn't going to make the same mistake his mother had made.

'OK, ladies. You're all ready—it's time to climb the magnificent Harbour Bridge!'

The girls tittered and giggled and they set off, led up the stairs by the climb leader. Only one woman remained behind.

'Come on, Brooke, we have to stick together—we're all joined.'

Finally Jack looked at Brooke's face. This wasn't just nerves. Real fear spread across her features. Brooke was scared and he couldn't just stand back and watch. Not when he knew how brave and strong she normally was.

'Brooke, what's wrong?'

Brooke didn't look at him. Her face had gone white and she was gripping the rails on either side of her.

'Nothing.'

'Brooke, it's OK. It's safe. You're connected by ropes. You can't fall.'

Brooke finally met his eyes. 'Yes, I *can* fall. It's too high. I can't do this,' she whispered.

Jack had never seen Brooke like this. She was genuinely frightened. He wanted to tell her not to do the challenge. He wanted to take her away and make her feel better, But he couldn't. The cameras were rolling. He shouldn't even be talking to her. But he couldn't leave her. He knew no one else would be able to help.

'You won't fall. I'll come with you. I'll stand right behind you.'

He could see in her eyes that she wanted to say no. She wanted to tell him she could do this on her own but the fear was clearly too much. She took one hand off the rail and grabbed his forearm, holding him tight. He reached out and held her arm, not once wanting to throw her hand off.

It had been over a week since he'd touched her. Over a week since he'd felt her skin. He missed it. He missed her. But he had to push all that away.

'Don't let me fall.'

Jack held on tight and let his gaze fix hard on hers.

'I won't.'

The view from the top was not what Brooke was expecting. She'd expected to open her eyes, look down and see death swirling beneath her. But when she opened her eyes she didn't see death—or near-death. She saw sky. Wide, blue sky. She felt the wind as it picked up her hair and the breeze as it tickled behind her ears, cooling her body.

'Just breathe it in.'

Jack's voice was calming her. Like it always did. But it shouldn't. His voice should mean danger and warnings and everything that was bad. But it didn't.

'Don't look down. There's nothing interesting there. Look up. Out there—past the city.'

Brooke looked up and saw the clouds as they moved slowly. She couldn't hear anything but Jack's voice, and the hum of the traffic below muffled the squeals and giggles and conversations around her. Jack moved a little closer. Not close enough to touch—he'd never do that. But close enough that she could feel him. Big and strong and solid. If she fell he'd reach out and stop her.

Brooke breathed in deeply. The air was different up here. Cleaner, crisper—but thinner. She needed to breathe again and again just to stop her heart beating so fast. She was angry with him for not calling. For forgetting about her. But the emotion running through her right now wasn't anger—it was fear.

'It's different to what I thought it would be.'

The city didn't look real from up here. It looked like an animation. A pretend city you'd see in a boy's train set.

'Everything looks different when you conquer something you thought you couldn't.'

'Wow.' Brooke whipped her head round to face Jack. 'Those are wise words from a self-confessed emotionless, indifferent, unfeeling, apathetic bastard.'

Jack blinked at her and twisted his mouth into a half-smile before looking out to sea, then back at her. 'Is that what I said?'

'Word for word.'

'You have a good memory.'

'Sometimes. When I know someone is saying something untrue and I want to use it against them later.'

'I should have known you had an ulterior motive.'

'Well, at least I put my motives on the table.'

'I think I've made *my* motives pretty clear.'

'You're right—your motives *are* clear.'

Jack blinked in the wind, his hair blowing across his forehead. His eyes were dark and set on her, making her feel unable to move. She wanted to reach for him, wanted to feel him hold her, but he just wanted to be friends. She didn't need a friend.

'I don't have motives, Brooke. I just want to get through the next few weeks of taping. That's all.'

That's all. That was all this had ever been about. The show. Ratings.

'That's right—you don't think, do you? It's all about you and what you want.'

His eyes didn't leave hers. 'Is that what you think of me?'

She was angry. She could feel it burning at her. But this time she wasn't going to let it out. She wasn't going to show it. She would find her Zen if it killed her.

Brooke gripped the rails and looked up. 'I don't think about you, Jack.'

It was a lie. A terrible, awful lie. But she had to lie because if she let the words she wanted to say out of her mouth she wasn't sure she'd be able to stop.

'Yes, you do. I know you do.'

'I don't.'

She looked at him then, straight into his eyes, refusing to believe that when her stomach flipped it was from anything but hunger. Refusing to believe that she could possibly smell him as she thought she could. They were hundreds of feet up and the wind was blowing. She couldn't smell *anything.* It must just be the memory of his scent. Because his scent had been all around her the other night and hadn't left her mind for the past three days.

Brooke thought of the other night. Again. She was hot now, and heavy, and she knew what she wanted. But she didn't want to remember his scent.

'You're nothing to me.'

Good. Cool. Nice response. He would have no idea what she was thinking. And that was a relief, because right now she was realising what it was about bad boys that women found so attractive.

It wasn't just their muscles and their tattoos and the dirty way they spoke, or the passionate, almost disrespectful way they pushed you down to kiss you. It was a pathetic female need to believe that inside every bad man was a *good* little boy, waiting for the right girl to find him. Which was complete rubbish. Jack wasn't good. He was bad. *Very* bad. She just needed to remember that— not his incredible sexy smell.

He didn't answer her and he didn't move.

'What's supposed to happen now?' Brooke moved away, still gripping the rail in front of her. 'Are we supposed to say how beautiful Sydney is? How much is Sydney Tourism paying you for this segment, Jack?'

She knew she was being cynical and flippant and rude but she had to be—because if she didn't she'd tell him what she really thought. And she wasn't going to do that. She wanted to get away from the memory of his smell and the flashing reminders of the way he'd kissed her and the words he'd growled into her ear that night. Of the way he'd made her feel as if she was the only woman he thought about and the only one he wanted.

No. She pulled her core in tight to stop the heat there from spreading. She needed to get the hell away from here. *Right now.*

'They're paying plenty. So you should take some photos, enjoy the view. Make it look as if you're having fun. You may as well settle in—we'll be here for another twenty minutes.'

'Then don't let me hold you up—I'm sure you have work to do.'

Jack leaned back to peer behind her. 'Nope, I'm good. Looks like Mick's got everything under control there.' There was a new anger in his voice now. As if he was holding back too.

Maybe if she didn't say anything he'd walk away.

'It's better up here, don't you think?' he said.

No, she didn't think that at all. Up here was beginning to feel a lot like torture. 'Mmm...'

'Nothing matters for a few minutes. You can just stop and breathe, you know...and think.'

She heard something in his voice. He was trying to tell her something but she had no idea what and she feared it was something she didn't want to hear. Some pathetic excuse. Some patronising brush-off.

Brooke breathed in. He was right. They were so far up and so far removed from anything it really *did* feel as if they were somewhere else and nothing else mattered. She had to calm down. She didn't want to hear what he had to say. She could tell he was angry too. Anger only got you into trouble.

Talk about something else. That would stop him from saying whatever it was he was going to say.

'When I was little I used to hide in a cupboard. It was dark and quiet and no one could find me. It was the only place I felt safe. That's what this feels like. Like I'm in the middle of everything but hidden away.'

'You hid in a cupboard?'

Crap. She shouldn't have said that. She needed to think of something else.

'Only a couple of times.'

'Why? I thought you and your sisters were best friends—why would you want to get away from them?'

Brooke licked her lips and lifted her hands to her hair, pulling it to one side. The anger was still there and it was starting to build again. 'We were…the cupboard-hiding business was…'

What was she *saying*? She needed to zip it.

'Was what?'

He was looking at her now. Intently. She could feel his dark eyes boring into her. Brooke tossed her hair, then gripped it again, pulling it into a ponytail at the back of her head.

'Well, it was…before.'

'Before?'

'Before I met my sisters.'

'You hid in a cupboard before you met your sisters?

Maybe it *is* time to go down, Brooke—clearly the air is too thin for you up here.'

He thought she was crazy. She knew she wasn't making any sense. But she didn't want him to think she was crazy—or angry.

Still pulling at her hair, she turned away from him. 'I didn't meet my sisters till I was six. I was adopted.'

The words came out soft, her lips barely moving. Her anger evaporated in an instant and was replaced with another emotion she hated even more. Sadness. Being adopted wasn't something she was ashamed of—it was just something she didn't like to talk about. People always asked questions. and she didn't like the answers she had to give.

But Jack was silent. He didn't ask any questions.

Brooke turned back. 'Did you hear me?'

'Yes.' He was still looking at her. His eyes dark, his long lashes still.

'Aren't you going to ask me about it?'

'No. Not unless you want me to.'

Not unless she wanted him to.

He *wasn't* considerate and lovely and thoughtful. Even though he'd taken away her anger in the sand the other night. Even though he'd helped her get up this damn bridge. Even though he was still here, talking to her, when she was saying things he didn't like. No, he was selfish and self-centred and he only wanted to be friends and didn't call. She was angry with him.

Brooke's mouth clamped shut and she turned back to the sky, resting her hands on the rail. Jack moved next to her, his elbows on the rail, fingers clasped—looking out at she wasn't sure what. They stood like that for a while. Not talking, not touching. Just looking.

Brooke wanted to tell him. She wanted to confide in

him. She missed her sisters, and she was lonely, and he was paying her attention so she wanted to tell him. She wanted to have this moment with him even if it was the only moment they'd ever have. Possibly *because* it was the only moment they'd ever have. After this was all over he'd be gone. It was safe to tell him.

'My birth parents put me up for adoption when I was five. I had to go to a foster home. I don't remember much—except that I would sit in a cupboard for hours. The old lady who was looking after me—Mrs Edwards, her name was—tried to get me to come out, but I didn't like her. I don't know why—looking back I'm pretty sure she was perfectly nice, but I hated her. So I hid in the cupboard.'

Jack still didn't say anything, but he turned to face her, one elbow still on the rail.

Brooke didn't look at him. She kept staring out to the ocean. 'One day she asked me if I wanted carrots with my dinner and I screamed and screamed at her, saying, *No! I don't want carrots!* That's all I remember saying—*I don't want carrots!* I was so angry.'

Brooke tried to smile. It sounded ridiculous now. But the smile kept disappearing, no matter how she forced her lips to move upwards. It wasn't funny. Not even now.

Brooke stopped and took a breath, pushing down the hard lump that was in danger of moving up from her chest into her throat. That had happened a long time ago. All that anger...all that hate. Brooke stared into the black water of the harbour below. When she spoke again her voice was quieter.

'She had all these porcelain cats everywhere and I started picking them up and throwing them. Smashing them. She grabbed me and tried to cuddle me but I fought her off. I threw the cats at her and they hit her in the head.

She was bleeding. There was so much blood. I remember all the blood.'

Still Jack remained silent. His silence was somehow comforting. She needed it. Slowly Brooke turned her body towards him. She still couldn't look at him, though, so she looked over his shoulder instead.

'I got moved then—to a house with two boys. I can't even remember their names. They didn't want me there. They would go off on their bikes super-fast so I couldn't catch up. They called me names. Sooky Brooky...The Girl That No One Wanted.'

Brooke felt Jack stand a little taller, his eyes still on her. She still couldn't look at him.

'One day I got angry because they were throwing rocks at me. I picked up the biggest one I could find and threw it back at them.'

Brooke pushed at her lips again and one of them managed to tip up half-heartedly. She looked down at her hands and picked at her nails. Something she hadn't done since she was a child.

'It hit one of them and he fell. He ended up in hospital.'

Brooke's heart stilled. Those boys had hated her. They'd told her that her father had got rid of her because she was too ugly and her mother hadn't wanted her because she couldn't do anything. But they didn't deserve what she had done. All because she'd got angry.

'Brooke...'

When Jack finally spoke his voice was deep and soft. As soon as she heard him say her name she wished he hadn't. It wasn't emotionless and indifferent and unfeeling at all.

She didn't look at him. She remembered those boys. She remembered the way they'd left her out and the way they'd only played boys' games and wouldn't let her join in. She remembered the boy splayed out in the dust. She'd thought she'd killed him. She remembered running away as fast as she could. They'd come and taken her away that night. She'd been so scared and so angry.

'Brooke. You were just a little kid.'

Brooke shook her head. She'd been a kid but she'd known what she was doing. She'd wanted to hurt them. The way she had hurt. Still hurt. The lump rose and Brooke choked it back down. She swallowed hard, trying desperately to stop the sob from falling out. She wasn't going to cry. Not about that. Not now—and not in front of Jack.

'Brooke.'

When his hands touched hers the sob stuck in her chest. He wasn't touching her the way he had the other night. It wasn't fast and hard and fleeting. It was firm, but tender. His fingers wrapped around hers, stopping her from picking at her nails. The air stilled for a moment and breathing became difficult. When Brooke looked up she met Jack's eyes. Dark and soft and full of concern. But almost as quickly as he came he went away. He pulled his hands back and shoved them in his pockets, breaking his gaze and searching the ocean for something.

'It's natural for someone to get angry when they're hurt.'

Brooke's heart jumped and started beating again. That small intimate moment had made the sob disappear. Somehow that second of recognition behind his eyes, the very small show of concern she hadn't been expecting, had given her whatever it was she'd needed to become unstuck from that memory and move on to another one.

'Getting angry doesn't solve anything.'

The burning behind Brooke's eyes stopped. She kept her eyes on him. On his nose and the way it jutted from his face. On the way he tilted his chin up almost defiantly. But mostly she watched the way his jaw was working… up and down and up and down… As if he was thinking and trying to hold back his own emotion. The idea that Jack could get emotional made her focus. Jack…? Emotional…?

'I hurt them because I was angry.'

'You were angry because they hurt you. I'm not saying you should have thrown things or made people bleed…'

He turned his dark eyes to her and held them steady. They were almost black. She didn't know him well enough to know what he was thinking, but he was definitely thinking *something*. What she'd said had affected him in some way and it surprised her.

'But sometimes you need to get angry. You need to let people know that you've had enough and you won't be treated like that. Sometimes you need to get angry so people know you're hurting and that you need help. And just think—if you hadn't got angry and done those things you never would have ended up with your sisters.'

The words of those boys still rang through her ears every now and again. So did visions of the old lady bleeding or the little boy lying in the dust. When something bad happened or when she was sad or lonely. But mostly they were drowned out by the things her sisters had said to her since. The good things and the happy things, the sweet things and the encouraging things. She knew how lucky she was to have her sisters. She'd seen what it was like to live without love, and the chaos and bickering she'd grown up with from her sisters was infinitely better. Without a doubt.

'Anger isn't always bad. It's just something we need to feel sometimes so we know what we don't want. Just like we need to feel sad so we can appreciate when we feel happy. You shouldn't be scared of how you feel.'

Jack was looking at her. For too long. His hands were still in his pockets and his eyes were on her. He was not touching, not coming close, just watching—almost warily.

'But *you* get scared, Jack. Maybe not of anger or sadness, but you're scared of getting close. Of being happy.'

There was something Jack wasn't saying. She needed to tread carefully here. If she was going to get him to reveal anything she'd need to be gentle.

Jack watched her, his eyes not leaving hers. She was right. He *was* scared of getting close. Scared of being happy. Because happiness never lasted. He'd known moments of it. Short, hard, fast moments of happiness that would disappear into puffs of smoke. It never lasted.

'Getting close means getting hurt.'

'Is that why you didn't call?'

Her face had changed. Her eyes dipped, then met his again. They widened, then she turned to look out at the water again. She was upset—he could see that. He hadn't meant to upset her. He'd meant to give her space. That time in the sand had just been comfort. She hadn't wanted more. He hadn't called because she didn't want more.

'What would I have said if I *had* called?'

Her head whipped back and she faced him, her green eyes bright and narrowed. She crossed her arms over her small body and stared at him, anger obviously simmering on the surface. 'How about, *How are you?* How about, *I'm thinking of you*? How about, *That meant something to me*?'

Her cheeks pinkened and her eyes challenged him. She looked beautiful. Petite and defenceless but Amazonian and capable all at once. He liked that about her. He liked her contrasts so much it made his chest ache. He wanted to know more—he wanted to reach out and touch her hot cheeks, he wanted to kiss her. But he didn't because he had no idea what she wanted. She was confusing and beautiful and it made his head spin.

Jack clung to the rail, planting his feet so he wouldn't sway. He had to just tell her. He had to just let her know what he was thinking. If his parents had taught him anything with their messed up fallacy of a marriage it was that he needed to say what he was thinking.

'*You* mean something to me.'

Brooke opened her mouth, then closed it. A line creased her forehead between her eyes. She opened her mouth again and closed it again. Her eyes remained on his, searching.

'What?'

'I think about you all the time. I think about your eyes and your smile, and I think about your gorgeous body and how it moved in the sand when I was kissing you.'

Brooke sucked in a deep breath.

He needed to stop. He had no idea what she was thinking, but he couldn't stop. Not now he'd started.

'I think about how you fight with me about everything and how you don't let me get away with anything. I think about that dimple in your left cheek.'

She let out a little puff of air and that dimple appeared. It swelled his brain. He had to keep going.

'I think about how you always say what you think, even when you know it'll probably get you into trouble. But the thing is—mostly I just think about *you*. Just you.'

Brooke stared. Then her hands flew to her eyes and she rubbed them, before taking them away and staring at him again.

'But you didn't call.'

'No. I didn't call. Because I didn't think you wanted me to.'

There—she had it all. It was on the table and now it was her turn. The idea filled him with a fear that made him go cold. He *never* gave his power away. He never gave anyone the ammunition to hurt him. But he'd given it to her. She'd give him the speech now. The 'let's be friends' speech. He hadn't heard that in years, because he'd always been the one giving it.

His stomach ached and his head hurt. He gripped the rail hard and held his breath.

Slowly, carefully, she moved her hand. It rested on his forearm and he shivered. Then she let her fingers trail down to his and he watched their journey. Her touch wasn't uncomfortable. It made his skin tingle. It made the hairs on the back of his hand stand up. But it wasn't uncomfortable. Exciting, erotic, electric—but not un-comfortable.

'I wanted you to call.'

'You didn't want to just be friends the other night?'

'No.'

Finally her fingers met his hand and she looped them underneath his palm. Relief coursed through his body.

'I didn't want to be friends. I wanted to be more than friends.'

More than friends? 'How much more?'

Her fingers moved until they were holding his hand tight. She stepped in closer and he felt her, warm and soft against his chest. He carefully moved his other hand till it was behind her neck. He pushed and she came closer. His body was hard and he wanted her there. Close and soft and pressing up against him. He moved forward until the whole length of him was pushed up against the whole length of her. Her free hand moved to his waist and curled around his back. She moved even closer, her breasts pushing against him and her hand pushing on his back.

Everything in his body screamed at the contact but he ignored it. He wanted her close, he needed to feel her, and he needed to feel the way she wanted him back. *More*. He could give her more. He could give her anything she wanted.

Her chin tilted up to him and her hair fell off her shoulders, tumbling down her back. He let his fingers thread though it—soft and fragrant. He leaned down to bury his face in her hair before finding her hot neck with his lips and kissing her. Tenderly, softly, and with a passionate reverence he hoped she'd be able to feel.

The low moan that escaped her lips was enough. His whole body fired to attention and the kisses on her neck became harder and faster and more desperate, until he'd kissed his way up to her mouth and was taking her in. Desperately kissing and moving to get as close as he could.

And then he realised she was doing the same.

CHAPTER TWELVE

'WHAT I REMEMBER…'

Max Douglas's voice boomed off the screen. This was Max at his bullying best. The veins in his forehead bulged through his reddened skin. Jack knew his own veins looked exactly the same.

'…is that you let your heart rule your head—even after everything I taught you. You let some woman manipulate you and change all the rules to suit *her*. And what happened in the end, Jack? She lied to you. She didn't want you. She wanted that other tosser. All that happened was that you caused an on-air fight that got us chucked off the air.'

Jack tried to breathe. Once again his father had got it wrong. No matter how many times Jack told him what had happened his father always preferred his own version of events. Jack hadn't been in love with Kayla. But she'd been young, and had seemed innocent and frightened and unsure what to do. So he'd helped her.

She'd said she was frightened of one of the other contestants—said he intimidated her when the cameras weren't there. Jack hadn't been able to have him thrown off the show so he'd adjusted the editing to 'out' the man, ensuring he would be voted off because of his bullying. What he hadn't known was that Kayla was in love with the bully and he'd rejected her advances. He'd made her feel small and unworthy. And then he'd started something with her on-screen best friend.

Jack should have known what a woman scorned in love was like. But he'd believed her. He'd wanted to protect her.

When the new edits had been shown the truth had come out: Kayla wanted her best friend's man. She'd lied and manipulated until she'd managed to get the man in bed and had waited till the cameras had caught them. She'd wanted her best friend's man and she'd got him—with Jack's help.

The other contestants had got involved—people had started taking sides—and when the punches and the hair-pulling had started things had got ugly. And it had all been caught on camera. Jack had thrown Kayla off the show but it had been too late—the TV authorities had shut the programme down, the company had lost millions, and Jack's father had nearly come through the phone line.

That had been five years ago. Jack had learnt his lesson. He'd learnt to keep everyone at a distance—that way he couldn't get sucked into any of their lies. Except now he'd let Brooke in. Was his thinking screwed up because of her? Were his father and Rob Gunn right? *Should* he let the men choose? He didn't know—and that made him angry.

But what made him angrier was his father on the line—telling him what to do. Overriding his decisions and making everything so much harder.

'This is *my* show, Max. I came up with the concept, I wrote the format, I got all the funding together and I handpicked the team. You're not going to take over.'

'I couldn't care less what you've done, Jack. You're wrong. I'm right. Gunn stays.'

'No. *You're* wrong. Gunn is banned from the set. If I see him again I'll have him escorted from the building and there's nothing you can do about it—unless you come here yourself, and we both know you won't do that.'

His father had been living in Italy for over four years now. He'd been home maybe five times. He'd told Jack's mother he was setting up a new company. Jack knew he was living with his mistress.

'I still own this company, Jack, and the last time I checked you were on my payroll. The format stays as is. The men choose the competitions. The men choose the women. The men control the show. The women are there for decoration and drama and if you don't like it you know where the door is. Be prepared to pay me back every cent. And don't think I won't come after your mother for it if *you* can't deliver.'

Jack's blood steamed. Not only was his father at his intimidating, bullying best, he was pointing out the very reason Jack couldn't leave. His father would target his mother if he did. But, he reminded himself, his mother could take care of herself. Or could she? And what would happen to Brooke and the others if he walked off the show?

No, he had to stay. He had to stay and try and protect Brooke and the others as well as he could. At least from within he could do something—if he left he would be powerless, and right now he was angry and he wanted to fight. For his mother, for Brooke, and against the man whose voice made him feel as if his hands were squeezing tight around his throat.

'You win, Max. You have me where you want me. I'll stay.'

* * *

When the girls received the envelope explaining the next challenge Brooke's heart sank. A cheer-off. Of all the demeaning, humiliating things…

The men had demanded they dress in skimpy cheerleader outfits and dance and sing and run around like chooks with their heads cut off. All for their amusement. How this determined who was their perfect match she had no idea. But she wasn't calling the shots—Jack was. The man who confused her more than anyone ever had.

After their mind-blowing kiss on the bridge they'd said goodbye with smiles full of meaning. He'd called the apartment the next day. Said he was thinking of her. She'd clung to the receiver so it wouldn't fall. Her heart had beat so fast she was sure the other girls would be able to see it.

Their conversation had been short—she hadn't been able to talk anyway, with the other girls listening in—and then she'd got mad, because she'd realised he was able to shift her emotions so severely. As if she had no control over them. She didn't want him to be able to control her like that but he did—and that made her angry. Except it was hard to be angry when she thought of his mouth and his kisses and the way he'd told her she meant something to him.

And now she gripped the envelope in her hand and her stomach rose to her throat as she thought about Jack making them do this. He surely knew how much she'd hate it? Did he not consider her feelings? Or were her feelings second to the ratings?

But one thing she'd learnt over the past few weeks was not to assume anything, and the moment she saw Jack she was going to sort this out. There was no way she and the other girls were going to endure a series of embarrassing challenges only to be chosen or rejected by four meat-heads who hadn't even taken the time to get to know them.

The night they'd been introduced the men had zeroed in on the women they'd clearly thought were the hottest, then got bored and spent the night talking to each other and drinking before disappearing. Probably to visit some seedy strip club and talk about what a sweet deal they had.

Heat rose from Brooke's legs up to her head. How *dared* they do this? How *dared* they assume that the twelve of them would just sit back and accept this new twist? If her sisters had taught her anything it was to respect herself and make her own choices. She wasn't about to let four strangers make her feel rejected or less than she was. And as she looked at the other women, still talking about the cheerleading challenge, she knew she wasn't going to let those strangers do it to these girls either.

Some of these women were vulnerable and shy and didn't have a lot of confidence to begin with. She wasn't going to let their confidence be shattered by a few bad men with perverted control fantasies. Jack had once said that anger could be a good thing, that you should speak up for what you believed in. She'd never thought about that before. She'd thought that anger always got you into trouble. That was why she'd spent years trying to keep her anger tucked away. Now she realised that anger could be good.

But instead of lashing out, and providing Jack with 'great TV', she needed to channel that anger into something much more productive. Like forming a plan to let these men—*and* Jack—know exactly what she and the other girls thought of their challenge. A plan to let them know who was really calling the shots on this show.

Brooke's body buzzed with the anger that flowed through her veins. She needed to release it—that was the only way she was going to survive this.

'Jack, it's humiliating!'

'Brooke. Listen to me—'

'No! You listen to *me*. We're not here to be humiliated and made to feel like pieces of meat. We won't do this.'

This time the girls were behind her. She'd spoken to them. They hated the idea of there being only four men. How were they supposed to meet their perfect match when there were only four men to choose from? They were united. They weren't going to take it. The girls were ready to rebel—they were just waiting for their fearless leader to give the word.

'You *have* to do this. Trust me—it could be a lot worse.'

'Worse? How? How could it be *worse*? We'll be on national television with our butts hanging out, dancing and chanting with no idea what we're doing! What are you hoping for—that we'll all fall and break our necks? That would be great TV, wouldn't it!'

Brooke stood up. She needed to be above him. She couldn't look into his calm eyes any longer. He wasn't getting roused at all. He wasn't even getting defensive. He was just sitting and watching her. She knew what he was doing—trying to calm her down. Well, she didn't want to be calm. He'd told her getting angry was good, so she was getting angry. She was going to test his theory. She had a plan.

She wasn't going to tell him about it, though. She had a plan to turn the tables on the men and let them know what the women all thought of their 'challenge' and the new rules. But that wasn't what was making her angry right now. It was Jack.

Was this who he really was? Where was the sensitive man on the bridge? Or the comforting man in the sand? This emotionless, unfeeling Jack infuriated her. She didn't want him.

'Brooke, I know you're angry, but you have to trust me.'

'Trust you? How can I trust you? What are you *doing*, Jack? This is ridiculous—and awful. How can you think this is OK?'

How can you think this is OK to do to me? She didn't say it, but she was thinking it—oh, was she thinking it!

'I *don't* think this is OK.'

'Then why are you letting it happen?'

'I have to. I have no choice. You have to trust me, Brooke—the first suggestion was a lot worse than this...'

'What do you mean, you have no choice? You're the producer!'

He didn't move. She watched him still, and then he retreated. His eyes blanked. He turned away.

'Jack. Tell me what's going on.'

'Just trust me, Brooke.'

He didn't reach for her. His hands stayed where they were. She knew what that meant. He wasn't touching her because he was feeling out of control. Keeping her at a distance was his way of regaining it. But this couldn't be about control. If they had a chance of working Jack had to realise that they were a team. He didn't have to do this on his own.

So she sat back down—this time next to him—and reached for his stiff hand. She curled her small fingers through his and didn't let go, even when he didn't squeeze back. She just moved closer.

'What's going on, Jack? Tell me.'

* * *

When Jack looked into Brooke's eyes he saw something he'd never seen before. Someone who wanted to know what was wrong with him. Someone who was concerned with what he was going through. Someone who was shattering his walls and wanting to see the man behind.

It made his chest ache. He felt exposed and uncomfortable, but he wanted her to keep looking at him like that. He wanted to feel her warm hand in his and he wanted her to smile again and then kiss him. So he told her. *Everything.* About his father and his mother and the deal he'd made when he was nineteen.

Brooke didn't speak. She just held his hand and listened as no one had ever listened before. When he'd finished he felt sick and completely exhausted. As if everything that he'd been keeping to himself was physically weighing down on him. He looked into her eyes, worried he'd said too much. Worried that she wouldn't understand.

But he shouldn't have worried. The fierce little nymph sitting next to him moved closer, her perfect breasts brushing his arm, her dimple getting deeper as she smiled, moving in closer to his ear. And when he felt the warmth of her breath on his ear as she whispered his whole body stood to attention.

'Sounds like it's time you got angry, Jack.'

The girls were buzzing. They'd been up half the night working out their routine, chanting the words and practising the lifts. For most it was hard work. Many of these women hadn't ever done anything more strenuous than running on a treadmill.

Despite being the least athletic in her family, Brooke excelled at the cheerleading routine. She was strong, so she could throw the other girls in the air and catch them with ease. She was also agile enough to flip when she was thrown up herself. She supposed that all those years of training had achieved something. Perhaps comparing herself to her sisters was not the best idea—they were freakishly good, after all—but compared with the rest of the population Brooke realised that her persistence and dedication had actually paid off. She was *good*.

They were all dressed in ridiculously brief outfits—although Brooke *had* managed to convince the wardrobe consultant to purchase everything from Wright Sports. Maddy was going to flip when she saw it all on screen.

For a moment Brooke wondered if her plan would perhaps show the brand in a bad light. But how could it? Standing up for themselves and turning the tables on men could never be bad. And if some people didn't like it then Brooke didn't care. She didn't want them as customers anyway.

One of the goals of Wright Sports was to promote women in sport. As professionals who demanded as much respect and money as their male counterparts. Her little cheer today would only help their cause. No—this was the right thing to do. Channelling her anger into a well-thought-out plan was a *good* idea. And Brooke couldn't wait for this thing to start.

The crowd at the football game was pumped. It was a big game—a fierce battle. Screams and whoops echoed around them as the girls stood waiting in the tunnel and the ground's announcer started to talk.

'Make some noise, everyone—we have over eighty-five thousand fans in the stadium tonight and we want to hear each and every one of you!'

The crowd howled in delight. Excitement turned to

flutterings in Brooke's stomach. She turned to the other girls and knew they were feeling the same.

Katy was looking a little green. She reached for her hand. 'We're going to nail this, Katy,'

'Do you think we're doing the right thing?'

'Yes, absolutely. One hundred per cent.'

Katy's eyes flickered with doubt. 'But what if one of those men actually is my perfect match?'

'Katy—look at me.'

Katy's big brown eyes stared into hers. Brooke saw her fear. She saw her doubt. She saw twenty-seven years of wondering if she was good enough. Wondering if she'd ever meet 'the one'. Wondering what she'd done every time it went wrong. Wondering if one of the men she'd let go because he'd treated her badly should have received a second chance.

'Your perfect match doesn't exist. That's not what it's about. It's about meeting someone who helps you on your journey. Who heals your heart and sees through your pain—who sees who you are and loves you anyway. Who holds you when you're sad and celebrates with you when you're happy. You'll meet that person when the time is right. And it may not last with that person, but then you'll meet someone else. And if you don't—it's OK. You'll have family and friends and people who love you and you'll be happy. Love isn't perfect, Katy—it gets messy and complicated because *people* are messy and complicated and we're all just muddling through together. There's no destination to get to. And there's no guarantee that finding the perfect man will make you happy. But I'll tell you something…'

Brooke reached up high to put her hands on Katy's shoulders before pulling her into a hug and whispering in her ear.

'The next five minutes *will* make you happy.' Brooke smiled. 'I promise.'

The loud voice of the announcer boomed across the field and into the tunnel. It was time. They were supposed to go out there, dance and cheer, and let four men they didn't even know assess their abilities and choose which one of them he wanted to go on a date with.

Brooke couldn't wait to see their faces. And she couldn't wait to see Jack's.

The girls rushed onto the podium in a hurry. Brooke called out to them to get ready. She looked each of them in the eye. They looked back. It was time. They were ready.

With a whoop and a cheer they began their chant while simultaneously flipping each other up and around.

You might be good at cricket
You might be good at that
But when it comes to football
You might as well step back
Might as well step back
Say what?

The crowd roared in appreciation and started to clap along. Brooke smiled as she flew into the air. They shouted louder this time.

You might as well step back
Cause we ain't gonna play no more
No, we ain't gonna play your way
Cause we're the girls of Perfect Match
And we're about to say
Say what?
We're about to say...

The girls stopped flipping. They formed a line. Their voices boomed through the microphones attached to their tiny crop tops.

You can take your silly cheering comp
Cause we think it's corrupt
Say what?
We hate to disappoint you
We hate to interrupt
But this is what we think of you
It's time you all got...

They turned, flipped up their skirts and bent over. An audible gasp filled the stadium and the clapping stopped. No one moved. Then suddenly there was a flurry of activity as photographers rushed from the sidelines to take photos of the girls butts. They stayed where they were.

Brooke turned her head. 'Done!' she called, and they stood up, turned around and faced the crowd, who had started to twitter.

They called out, then clapped, and finally they roared and cheered. Relief rushed through Brooke's body. They *got* it. They understood.

Brooke clasped the hands of the girls either side of her and squeezed and then, holding their hands aloft, the girls took their bows before bouncing offstage as if they'd just been fed a truckload of red frogs.

The conversation Jack was having with his father that afternoon wasn't pretty. His father was roaring. He wanted to know who had organised it. He wanted heads to roll and blood to be spilled. He blamed Jack, of course, and Jack was taking great pleasure in the rant his father was giving him.

'Which one was it?' his father demanded, the angry purple veins in his neck popping. 'It was the little one, wasn't it? Tell me! It was her, wasn't it? She's been causing trouble from the beginning. You need to get rid of her!'

Jack's throat closed. His father couldn't get wind of Brooke's having anything to do with this. The thought of his father saying anything to her made his body fill with a rage he hadn't felt in years. Not since he'd found out about his father's first girlfriend.

'The girls were never going to put up with this, Max, you had to expect rebellion.'

'If I find out it was her she'll be sorry she ever opened her stupid little mouth…'

'That's enough, Max.'

Jack's blood pumped. *Calm.* He had to stay calm. He couldn't let his father know how he felt about Brooke. If he knew Brooke would pay…big-time.

'It's not enough. That small-titted little troublemaker had better watch herself. I can make her life miserable— you tell her that.'

Jack stood up. White spots danced before his eyes. 'First of all, you don't speak about her like that. And second—if you hurt her in any way I will hunt you down, Max, and you'll be the one who's sorry.'

As soon as the words left his mouth he regretted them.

'Geez, Jack, don't tell me you're having a fling with her? Is *that* what this is about? You've let *another* woman manipulate you?'

'I'm not having a fling with anyone.' That was true. Brooke was not a fling. 'But you're not going to threaten *any* of the contestants like that. I'm still in charge here.'

'If I find out you've become involved with this girl…'

Jack had to dig himself out. He couldn't let his father

know—couldn't let his father turn his anger and hatred on Brooke. That wasn't going to happen.

'I'm not. Do you think I'd send her on a date with the biggest jerk on the show if I was involved with her?'

Jack was thinking on his feet. He wasn't sure if he was doing the right thing, but right now he just had to steer his father off-course.

'Brent?'

'Yes. I've teed it up for Brent to choose her. She'll hate it. It'll make great TV.'

It would. But what would make greater TV was what she was going to say to him after that date. Brent was the most stupid, sexist loser Jack had ever met. All muscles, no substance. Brooke would hate him. And hate Jack for setting them up. But he had to get his father off the trail. He wouldn't be able to stand what would happen to her if he didn't.

'Nothing had better go wrong this time, Jack. Get it together. I'll pull it off the air myself if *anyone*—including that troublemaker—does anything to jeopardise our ratings or the show's future. Do you understand?'

Jack understood. He understood that he'd had enough. He was getting out. He'd pay his father back any way he could, but after this show was done and Brooke was safe—he was out.

'I choose Samantha Draper.'

'I choose Dimity Lee.'

'I choose Brooke Wright.'

The whole room fell silent. In their wisdom, the powers-that-be had decided that the dates would be doled out on a boat in Sydney Harbour. Brooke suspected it was so no one could run.

They were dressed in full formal regalia. They'd been

in make-up for hours, getting their hair to sit just right and creating the perfect winged eyeliner. Brooke had never felt less like herself. When she looked in the mirror a stranger stared back. A beautiful stranger—but someone Brooke didn't recognise. False eyelashes hovered over her eyes—she longed to rip them off.

Someone shifted. The women were standing in a row on the top deck of the boat, their backs to the magnificent Harbour Bridge. The four men stood before them, smiling in their suits. One leered at her. He'd just called out her name.

A gust of wind blew a strand of hair into Brooke's open mouth. Someone had chosen *her*? Why? He was smiling at her. Big and muscly, clearly a bodybuilder. *So* not her type. He was dressed in baggy jeans and he had a flat cap on his head. Clearly he was trying to look younger than he was—she was sure he was bald underneath that cap he never took off.

He held out a brawny hand to her and she took it, wondering what this meat-head saw in her. His eyes trailed over her body and she knew.

'You looked hot out there today, Brooke.'

Brooke didn't answer him. She turned back to the other girls, who offered a few sympathetic smiles.

What the hell had she got herself into?

The date started badly. His name was Brent and he was thirty. Although he dressed as if he was twenty-one. He laughed a lot, but conversation clearly wasn't one of his strengths. His biceps bulged out of his too-small shirt. A faint smell of fake tan lingered around him.

'Your arse looks hot in that dress.'

Brooke gulped down the water she'd just taken a swig of. He'd chosen an oceanside bar for their date. It was

packed, but the producers had managed to set up a se-
cluded set of stools for them so they could tape without
too much noise. Brooke had a headache from the thumping music and her patience was incredibly thin as she
watched this thick-head eye up every woman who walked
past in a short skirt.

'Thank you. Your biceps look ridiculous in that shirt.'

He laughed uncertainly, clearly not sure if she was
joking. She wasn't.

'What do you want to eat? This mob are payin', so
order as much as you want.' He smiled.

The man was attractive—she'd give him that. Nice
teeth. A wide jaw. He was manly-looking. Big and handsome. But it was his personality she was struggling with.
Or rather she was struggling to find one.

'What do you do, Brent?'

Brent's head turned as another pretty young thing
walked past.

'I'm a project manager.'

Brooke rolled her eyes. If she had a dollar…

'So you're a tradie?'

'Ah…yeah, I s'pose you could say that. I'm a sparkie.'

An electrician. Good job. Steady. Reliable work. OK—
one good thing.

'And where do you live?'

'Bondi.'

Brooke smiled, waiting. But the silence was long-last-
ing. He sipped on his drink and pulled out his phone.
Brooke waited while he checked it, quietly annoyed that
he was able to have contact with the outside world while
she couldn't.

'What made you come on this show?'

'What is this? A police interview? Just relax, darl, and
enjoy your drink.'

Brooke felt frustration swell in her chest. So he didn't want to talk… What the hell were they going to do till the food arrived?

'I'm in marketing.'

He didn't look up but he grunted a little. The waitress came to take their order and he finally put his phone away, slipping it into his back pocket. Brooke was actually in pain now. This was without doubt her number one worst date *ever*.

'Are you looking for love, Brent?'

'Geez, slow down. You're pushy!' Brent took another sip of his drink and pulled out his phone again.

Brooke felt heat rise in her head. She could hear it fizzing in her ears. 'Look, mate. I don't know why you asked me on this date. You don't want to talk—you just want to check your phone and every girl who walks past. Clearly I'm not your "perfect match", so what are we doing here?'

Brent looked up and for the first time looked into her eyes. 'Jack said so.'

A breath expelled from Brooke's chest. *Jack?*

'What do you mean? I thought you chose me?'

'You're hot and all that, babe, but Jack told me to pick you. He said we'd be a perfect match. Look…' He leaned in to whisper in her ear. 'I have a girlfriend, but I'd be willing to forget her for one night if you want to have some fun.'

Brooke closed her eyes. She breathed deeply. *Don't go off,* she coached herself. *Don't go off.* This is what Jack wants. *Great TV.* Brooke going off about something else. Brooke being humiliated on national TV. *Don't go off— that's exactly what he wants.*

Every time she thought she had him figured out— every time she thought she'd got through to him—he did something else to make her anger flare her.

'Thank you for the lovely date, Brent, but I have to go.'

'Not yet! We haven't even eaten! I'm starving!'

'You stay, tiger. Eat all you want. I have somewhere I need to be.'

Brooke moved fast. Her feet barely hit the ground.

She grabbed the cameraman by the arm. 'Turn it off. *Now*. And take me to Jack.'

She was mad. A white rage had made spots appear before her eyes.

The cameraman didn't argue. He put down the camera and took her to his car.

CHAPTER THIRTEEN

SHE WAS HERE and she was angry—that much he could tell. And he knew *why* she was here. The unwatched footage sat leering at him on the computer screen. Mick had just emailed it over. Mick's promise of it being a great scene rang in his ears.

He wanted to watch. Not for the scene. Not for the drama. But he wanted to know. How had her date gone? Somewhere in his jealous heart he was worried that she might have enjoyed her date with that meat-head.

'Open the door, Jack. I'm not going anywhere until you do.'

Definitely angry.

Jack's heart leapt ridiculously. Maybe the date hadn't gone well. Maybe she'd realised the man was a jerk and she'd given him a serve and now she was here to declare her feelings for him.

Jack stepped back. No, she was angry. He knew what she was here for. To tell him off for forcing her to go on a date with Brent. She'd hate him. She wouldn't want 'more' from him now. But he'd had to do it—it was the only way Jack's father would leave her alone.

Reaching the video entry system, he swiped the screen to allow her face to show. 'What's wrong, Brooke—what are you doing here?'

Her face turned to the camera. 'Let. Me. In.'

She was mad. Madder than ever. And he knew he had to let her in. He *wanted* to let her in. She was angry and she needed to yell at him and, strangely, he wanted her to. He wanted her to take her anger out on him—as if he could absorb it for her and ease her pain.

Two short minutes later Jack opened the door to reveal Brooke. Dressed in a body-hugging black dress and pushing her way past him.

'This is *it*, Jack. The very end. I'm not putting up with this any longer. You've had your fun—I want out.'

'Brooke—'

Her arms were folded tight across her chest, making her breasts rise up and peep out from the top of the dress. Her cheeks were flushed and her hair was pulling free from the tight style she had it in. She looked angry and beautiful all at once.

'Don't "Brooke" me. I *know* what you did. I know why you chose Brent. You wanted the exact type of man that would annoy me the most. A misogynistic, stupid man-slut who has no self-worth and absolutely no idea how stupid he is.'

'Are you talking about your date, Brooke?'

'Yes, I'm talking about my date! The big knuckle-dragging caveman *you* set me up with. He spent all night checking out every other woman in the place. Then he suggested we go back to his place after they finished the taping because his girlfriend was away. You couldn't have found a more repulsive man and you know it.'

'I didn't know he had a girlfriend.'

'But you *did* know he was a pig? You told me that you wanted the best for us. That you really cared about us finding our perfect match. But you don't, do you? You just want to make entertaining TV.'

'I thought you liked the bodybuilder type.'

'Since when do I go for the stupid bodybuilder type? Since when do I seem like the type of woman who puts up with a man who thinks monogamy is a pizza topping? You don't know me at all and neither does anyone on your team. Do you even know what you're doing? Maybe your father was right and they *should* have brought in that hotshot producer. Maybe *he* would have found a man who was even close to being my type.'

'I thought you didn't want to find a man? I thought this was all about your family's business?'

'It is...' She hesitated, looking away.

She wanted a man. She was *disappointed*. Something burned hot in his gut and he knew what it was: jealousy. Stupid, worthless jealousy—for a man who wasn't even worth her notice.

'Is that the problem, Brooke. Did you get all excited when you saw Mr Muscles and hope he was the one for you? What happened?'

Brooke's eyes were wide and to his horror they were filling quickly with tears. He'd hit a nerve and he knew it, and he wished he could take back the stupid thing he'd just said.

'He has a girlfriend. He just wants to have some fun. He told me you told him to choose me, so I left.'

'Good.' *Good.* He felt better, but his chest was still pumping with blood. 'That's what you should have done.'

'He was a pig, Jack. He was mean and thoughtless and stupid and completely out of touch with the real world— and you sent him to me. You chose him for me.'

He had. She was right. He'd known they wouldn't go well together. He'd known she would hate him and he'd sent him to her. He shouldn't have done that. He should have found another way. Because now she was upset and it was his fault and he felt as big as an ant.

'Brooke, that's not what I—'

'Not what you *what*? Meant to do? You didn't mean to hurt me? Well, you did. You humiliated me and you treated me like any contestant on the show and you've never done that before. You treated me like I was a puppet to be manipulated and you made me feel used and dirty and stupid—and now I can't trust you.'

But that was what she'd signed up for. She knew that. She had to expect that. She *was* a contestant. This *was* a TV show. So why did he feel so small?

His chest with heaving with the heavy breaths he was taking. She wasn't just mad at him—she hated him. He could see it in her eyes, in the way she didn't come anywhere near him. Brooke always wanted to touch, she always came too close, but right now she was as far away from him as she could be and it made him feel cold and desperate. Desperate because he'd pushed her too far.

And the desperation that was prickling like a cold heat all over his body was a feeling a lot like something he hadn't felt in a long time. *Love*. He saw it in a flashing instant. He loved her. He wanted to protect her because he loved her. And that thought scared the hell out of him.

'You *are* a contestant, Brooke. That's what you're here for.'

The look she flashed him made his whole body go cold. *Hate*. Hate and disappointment and utter repulsion. The breath stopped in his throat. He sucked in air through his nose.

Time ticked by slowly. She stared at him, her eyes darting around his face as if trying to read him. Then they were still, and the mouth that had been held in a tight white line moments earlier opened.

'That's good, Jack. I needed to hear that. I needed to know what I am to you and how you really feel about me. I needed to be reminded what a selfish, narcissistic man you are before I started believing that you were actually one of the good guys. But you're not, are you? You're just as bad as the knuckle-dragger. No—you're worse. At least *he* was obvious about it. He let me know what a pig he was up-front. But you're stealthy, aren't you? You come across all sympathetic and kind and thoughtful, make me think you actually feel something for me—but it's just lies. You are a *liar*, Jack.'

Brooke had felt her body shake as she delivered her speech. She watched his face—unmoving and unemotional—as she spewed out her feelings. As she put everything out on the floor, waiting to see what he would pick up. But he didn't move. He just stood there. As if she were a stranger in the street. As if they hadn't shared the moments they had and as if they hadn't...

She'd wanted more from him—but not now. Now she was glad she hadn't let herself get carried away, because she knew if they'd gone further she would have let herself fall and she'd be feeling even worse than she was already.

'I told you before. I'm bad news.'

He delivered his statement so quietly she almost didn't hear him.

She wanted to walk out. His coldness and the way he wasn't even trying to apologise or salvage anything was hurting her physically. She wound her arms tighter to her body, pinching herself under her arms.

'So that's it? You just absolve yourself from any responsibility by saying you're bad news? You warned me so it's *my* fault when I get hurt? There's low, Jack—and then there's you. For you to deliberately hurt me—delib-

erately want to humiliate me—makes me think you're so
much more than bad news.'

She wasn't sure how she could hurt him as much as
he had hurt her but she wanted to. She wanted that fro-
zen look on his face to change. To something. *Anything.*
Anger, even—she didn't care. She just wanted him to
react—to acknowledge that he'd hurt her.

She let out a little huff of ironic laughter, searching
for the most hurtful words she could find. Her mind was
blank. She could only tell him how she felt—it was all
she had left right now.

'You're worse than your father. You are possibly the
most horrible person I've ever met. No. Not possibly.
You *are.*'

His face didn't move. She waited for his reaction—his
anger—but there was none.

She opened her mouth again. 'You're disgusting. I
know why you're single now, Jack—you're a horrible,
horrible person and I hate you.'

The words came without her thinking. She didn't even
mean them any more, but a blinding need to hurt him
had taken over her brain and her mouth.

'I feel sorry for the people who work for you and I feel
sorry for your family and anyone who has to put up with
you. You're cold and mean and a terrible person. I hate
you and I wish I'd never met you and I *definitely* wish I'd
never kissed you and I'm glad we didn't become friends
or anything else. You make me sick.'

Finally Brooke took a breath. The fog cleared and she
tried to remember what she'd said. Still Jack stood before her, starting at her. Unmoving. Her heart hurt. Her
arms hurt where she was pinching them. Everything hurt
and nothing she was saying was working. She needed to

leave. *Now.* She wanted to see her sisters and not to feel like this any more.

But just as she unfolded her arms to move she felt him. He moved quickly and he was in front of her, not touching, but standing so close she couldn't move. When she looked up his face was still hard, his mouth turned down at the edges, but his eyes were different. They were hot and angry and set on hers.

'Are you finished?' he asked, his voice a low, threatening growl.

He was too close and he stood over her. She didn't feel scared of *him* but she did feel scared. She'd wanted this reaction. She'd finally made him feel something—that was what she'd wanted. He felt…what? Anger? Something… This was just what she'd wanted but right now she wasn't sure if she'd done the right thing. Her mind flicked back to what she'd said. She couldn't be sure of every word but she knew she hadn't meant most of it. She'd just wanted him to react and now he had.

'You're angry, Brooke. *Good.* Get angry. Get angry at that jerk who didn't deserve you—get angry at me.'

Her breathing was now so heavy her breasts were moving up and down against his chest. She didn't answer him right away—she'd used up all her words and she just wanted to look at him. She wanted to watch his reaction. She wanted to know if he was as angry as she was.

The answer came seconds later when she felt his mouth, hot and hard against hers. His tongue pushed against her lips violently. His teeth nipped and he pushed at her, his arms coming around her back to pull her closer. Brooke pulled back, shocked, but he didn't let her go. For a second their eyes met, and she saw the anger in them before he closed them and set about kissing her again. Even harder. Even more passionately.

They weren't nice, loving kisses. They were genuine I-hate-you kisses. She felt his hate and his anger and his need to hurt her. She felt it in his lips and in the way he flicked his tongue as if the pleasure was all his. She wanted to push him away. She hated him even more. He had hurt her and she didn't want him to think she wanted this. But for some perverted reason she did. She wanted him pushing against her and kissing her and her stupid brain wouldn't let her pull away.

She pushed her lips closer, pushed her hips and her breasts and everything she had closer to him, snaking her hands up to his big shoulders and gripping them tightly, digging her fingernails in hard. His free hand moved up to her cheek and he cupped it as he kissed her, deeper and deeper, pushing her back further and further, till she was against the wall.

Before her brain could even register what was going on her body had reacted and she'd hoisted herself up, straddling his waist, which made him push her even harder into the wall. She felt him, long and hard against her, and moved her hand down till she felt him through his jeans. A deep growl escaped from his mouth and he left her lips for a second so he could kiss her neck, underneath her ear and further down. But these weren't gentle kisses either. They were hard, and he sucked as he went, his hands expertly moving behind her back to unclip the clasp on her bra.

There was no stopping now. She knew that. She accepted that. She didn't want to stop. She needed him close. She wanted to hurt him—to make him feel the violence of her kisses. When his face moved back up to hers she didn't give him time to look into her eyes. She kissed him again, biting his bottom lip and sucking it in, letting him know that she hated him as much as he hated her.

'I know you don't hate me, Brooke.'

His voice murmured in her ear as he kissed her neck. Brooke's blood was running hot and heavy. She *did* hate him. So much.

'I do hate you.'

'You don't hate me.'

He didn't stop kissing as he spoke. His hands explored her body and she responded with a loud moan as she arched into his touch.

'I do. You won't give me what I want.'

'What *do* you want?'

Jack pushed her skirt up and out of the way. His fingers explored beneath her underwear. She felt him gently sliding against her wetness.

'That—I want that.'

She wanted that. She wanted him. She wanted comfort. She wanted everything he had to offer.

Brooke kissed him hard. She bit his lower lip and he responded by pushing her against the wall. Her legs clung to him. She pushed into him. Angry and sad that she couldn't get what she wanted. Annoyed that she even wanted it. She should have known better than to fall for the wrong man.

Jack kissed her back, just as hard, and with the strength she knew he had lifted her up against the wall. She clawed frantically at his buttons. She needed to feel his skin. And when her hands found what they were looking for relief rushed to her head. She let her hands wander across his muscles and up to his shoulders as his large palms wrapped around her thighs and pulled her closer to him.

Their mouths didn't stop. Not for a second. When he wasn't kissing her mouth he was kissing her eyelids, or her neck, or her jaw, and she threw her head back to allow him access to every part of her. The only sound was the heavy breaths they took and her groan of pleasure as he finally removed her underwear.

Finally they paused. Made eye contact. This wasn't just sex. Couldn't be just sex. She wanted more, and when she looked at him she knew it *was* more.

He lifted a hand, dragged his thumb across her bottom lip, then kissed her. Long and hard and deep. Brooke forgot to breathe. She kissed him back, forgetting the sex, forgetting everything else except that kiss and the way they seemed to be drinking each other in, taking away each other's anger and leaving themselves with something more pure. Something much deeper.

By the time he pulled back she was ready. She had to have him. With a quick movement he was naked from the waist down and pushing on her, asking for permission. Which she gave, with a push and a long, hard slide.

Brooke couldn't help it. Her head flew back and the moan was out of her mouth before she could even think to stop it. His noises were much deeper, much more guttural, and they came from the back of his throat.

She focussed on the noise, on the way he was sliding up and down, and then on how he was using one finger to circle her clit before plunging into her again. She kissed his neck, now clammy with sweat, kissed his jaw, until finally she put her mouth over his and let her kisses match his strokes, faster and faster and deeper and deeper, until she felt it burst and shatter and she had to tell him to stop.

He stilled. He wasn't done. He hadn't finished and he wasn't going anywhere. He shifted as she shook and she held tight, not *wanting* him to go anywhere.

'Is that what you needed?' he growled into her ear.

'Yes. That. *Again.*'

She moved to allow the sparks to subside and then

start all over again. She was sensitive, and her orgasm sat right at the surface, so when he started to slide again she felt herself shudder and shake. But he didn't stop. He kept going. Pushing and going deeper, pausing to look down—clearly turned on by what he was seeing. She looked too, and watched as he slid in and out. Her fire sparked again. So close to the surface. But she didn't have time for release because it was his turn and he pushed into her with a force she wasn't expecting, banging her head on the wall behind her.

'Ouch!'

'Sorry…sorry!' His eyes were glazed but his hand came up to cradle the back of her head.

She felt his legs buckle a little, but he held her up. She lifted a hand to cover his on the back of her head. Warm, big… She put her small hand over his and he met her eyes.

'I'm sorry,' he whispered, his voice deep and hoarse.

'I know,' she whispered back, waiting for him to let her drop. But he didn't let her go. He wrapped his big arms around her and she buried her face in his warm skin, breathing in his scent and placing soft, tender kisses on his biceps.

They stood naked and silent for minutes before Brooke pulled away, brushing the hair from his forehead where it had fallen. She lifted herself up onto her toes and kissed his lips. This kiss was different. Soft and tender. He'd taken away her anger. He'd let her rage and allowed her to release herself without judgement. Without argument. And she was grateful for that. She'd needed that. She'd needed *him*.

'That was a bad thing you did, Jack.'

'I know.'

His voice was soft and she felt it travel through his chest and into hers.

'Are you going to tell me why you did it?'

She watched him, watched his eyes, sure he was going to tell her. That he had a plan. That sending her on that disastrous date had a hidden meaning she didn't know about. Maybe hoping that he'd sent her on a date with that dope so she wouldn't fall for anyone else. Because he wanted her to himself.

It couldn't be for ratings and great TV. She understood him now. She knew about his father and what he was making him do. All she wanted was to know that they were in this together. But he didn't say anything. He just shook his head.

'No?'

He still didn't say anything. Just lifted a hand to her hair and pushed it back, away from her face. It was a tender movement that didn't make any sense when he still wasn't letting her in. Brooke felt she was on a rollercoaster. Up and down, frightened and happy, exhilarated and angry—and right then, after what had happened, she just couldn't take it.

Brooke pushed against him till he released her. As she righted her clothes and retrieved her handbag from the floor a weakening sadness spread over her. Would Jack ever give her what she needed? Would he ever really get rid of that wall he'd built up in front of himself and let her in? Trust her?

'Brooke. Don't go yet.'

He didn't reach for her, just stood with his hands by his sides. Brooke looked into his eyes. More sadness. He was sad too. But, as much as he was sad, he wasn't offering her any more.

'I have to, Jack. I'm afraid my broken old heart can't

handle this. I don't know why you're holding back, and I don't know why you don't trust me, but you don't. I don't think you ever will. And I can't just have meaningless sex with you—I like you too much.'

'I can't tell you what's going on, Brooke.'

'Yes, you can. But you won't. And if I'm not on your team, Jack, I'm on the other side.'

She didn't wait for his reaction. She just turned, took a deep breath and walked out through the door.

CHAPTER FOURTEEN

WHEN THEY FINALLY reached the peak Brooke was panting. Sweat dripped down her neck and between her shoulder blades. It had to be almost forty degrees. Everything on her was hot and she needed a drink. The girls around her were sighing and breathing heavily too. They were exhausted.

The last day had come. The last challenge was over. And Brooke was so relieved she almost felt like crying. But she didn't have time to cry, because in the distance was a table laden with food and drinks, and standing around the table were some men.

Brooke counted them. Twelve. One for each woman. Who *were* these men? The girls started to twitter in excitement. Brooke felt an arm loop through hers and her stomach started to swirl as well. What was going on? Weren't they done?

After last night's party Mick had come to see them. He'd said they only had one more challenge left. He'd said the men would then make their choice. The challenge was supposed to be a hike to the top of the Curl Curl peninsula. Mick had said nothing about anyone else being there.

Brooke couldn't ask Jack. She wasn't even sure where Jack was. Typically, Jack hadn't been in contact. She missed him. She wanted to know how he was and what the hell was going on. But, as usual when it came to Jack, she was left in the dark. And now there was a crowd of people waiting for them.

What was going on *now*?

Brooke was exhausted. Physically and mentally. She was confused and starting to feel angry again. Angry that Jack was leaving her in the dark and frustrated that she was so close to seeing her sisters again but still so far away.

As they walked closer the girls' steps started getting faster. Excitement was starting to build. There were about ten cameras facing them as they climbed the last of the slope and came to the table and the strange men.

'Oh, no.'

Someone stopped.

'You can't be serious.'

Brooke looked around. Some of the girls had gone white. They didn't look happy. Brooke turned back to the table and squinted in the sun. She scanned the faces of the men until finally one of the faces registered. Brooke's blood rushed cold in her veins. Pinpricks touched her skin in a rush. *That face.* That wasn't a strange man. That was the man she'd hoped never to see ever again. *Mitch.* Standing behind the table. Smiling. At her.

Brooke wanted to run. She wanted to get the hell out of here and away from that face. But she couldn't. The cameras were close now, and all but two of the women had stopped. Those two had rushed to the table and embraced two of the men waiting. But the other women didn't.

Brooke realised what this was. Everyone's exes were here. *Great TV.* What better finale than forcing the women to come face to face with the men who had led them even to come on this ridiculous show? The drama was sure to be top level.

As she finally reached the table Mitch smiled at her. A smile that had once been so familiar and dear to her. Now it just seemed as if he was mocking her.

'Brooke. You look great!'

He was talking to her. How *dared* he talk to her? Around her, things were not going well. Someone was crying. There was shouting at one end of the table. Most of them were stiff and unsure.

'What the hell is going on? Why are you here, Mitch?'

'It's all about moving on, Brooky. I'm here to release you, so you can move on.'

Brooke's ears burned and she gripped the chair in front of her. 'Excuse me?'

'They thought it would be a good idea if you faced your demons. If you met up with the men you'd loved the most and had the chance to talk.'

'*They?* Who is they?'

Mitch's eyebrows furrowed. 'The people in charge— I don't know.'

Jack. Jack was in charge. Jack had arranged this.

Brooke didn't want to believe it. As she listened to the words coming out of Mitch's mouth she thought maybe it had been Mick's idea. Or even Jack's father's. But it hadn't. Jack had done this. Jack had sent Mitch back to her. *Jack.* Who knew what Mitch had done. Who knew how Mitch had made her feel. Why would he do this?

A woman's voice boomed out across the table.

'Ladies and gentlemen, it's time to sit. Today is all about breaking bread with someone from your past who has caused you pain. The aim is to get everything out in the open so you're able to move on to your own *Perfect Match.*'

People started to sit, but Brooke didn't want to sit. She wanted to leave. But then she saw the cameras. She wasn't going to make a scene. That was exactly what Jack wanted. That was exactly what Mitch wanted.

Why would Jack do this? How had she got him so wrong? How had she thought he was different? He *wasn't* different. This was all about ratings to him. And it didn't even matter if the show did end—Jack would always put success above her. She realised that now. This dirty trick had shown her the truth. Jack wasn't true and sincere. Jack would do anything to get what he wanted. Right now—he wanted a reaction. Well, Jack could go jump.

Brooke sat down and piled food on to her plate. Her appetite was gone but she was determined to eat and smile and pretend that none of this mattered.

'How have you been, Brooky?'

Mitch's voice had a high-pitched twang to it that she never noticed before. It irritated her. She shoved a piece of bread in her mouth and chewed.

'Don't talk to me, Mitch. Don't make polite conversation,' she hissed through the food and through her teeth. 'Just sit there and shut up.'

Mitch stopped eating. 'You know, Brooke, that was always the problem with you. You were always telling me what to do.'

What? The man had a hide. She'd never told him what to do. Perhaps she should have. He might have treated her better. Brooke remained silent. She didn't want to fight. She didn't want any reason for the camera to come her way.

'Still cold, Brooke? Still not letting anyone in?'

Brooke told herself to breathe. Cold? Her? She'd given Mitch *everything*. All of her. She'd been there for him when he was down. She'd pumped him up when his ego was low. She spent all her time and all her energy on him and then he'd left. As if she hadn't mattered. He'd replaced her and moved on.

'You know, Brooke, if you talked to me instead of projecting all this anger we might be able to work things out. I still care about you, you know.'

The spots of anger were back in front of Brooke's eyes. Her breathing was shallow. She sucked in a breath and chewed the remains of her bread.

'If your sisters butt out, that is.'

Brooke put her hands to her eyes and rubbed. She knew what she was about to do and she couldn't stop herself. She'd had enough.

Brooke stood up and banged her hands on the table. 'Ladies, this is *enough*. We've gone through enough. We don't have to sit here with these...men. These people who didn't understand us, didn't care about us. We are the authors of our own stories—not these sad excuses for men here at the table.'

'You're right, Brooke. I don't want to eat with you, Grant. I don't even want to look at you. I don't like you. I don't think I ever did.'

'And I won't sit across from *you*, knowing how many times you cheated on me. How many times you lied to me, Patrick.'

Alisssa's voice rang out across the table. 'And you know what, Matthew? I *did* cheat on you. You want to know why? Because you're bad in bed!'

Another woman stood and said her piece, then another, and another. Then it was Brooke's turn.

'You listen to me, Mitch, you little weasel. My sisters *knew* what a lying, cheating arse you are. They tried to warn me but I didn't listen to them. I believed *you*. And you betrayed me. You took everything I gave you, sucked up all my goodness, and then you walked away. You humiliated me and you treated me like I meant nothing. You are low, Mitch. Lower than low. But you're not my demon. You're nothing to me now. I don't even think about you, except to think how lucky I was to get away from you. I don't like you, I don't love you, and I've realised I never did. You were what I needed at that time in my life. But I don't need you any more. I don't need *any* man. I deserve to be treated with respect. I deserve a man who isn't afraid to love me madly and deeply. And I am way too good for you. I won't sit with you, Mitch. You don't deserve my time.'

By now she knew all the cameras were on her and she didn't care. Mitch needed to know that she wouldn't be treated like this. He needed to know that she was angry and that she was done. Done with bad men and bad relationships. And right now she needed to tell another man that too, because she was angry and she was worth it and *she* was calling the shots around here.

CHAPTER FIFTEEN

JACK GRABBED HIS bag and headed for the door. The taxi was here. He had waited as long as he could. He knew they were still taping the last scene. He'd tried to tell himself to stay away but he couldn't. He couldn't stand the thought of Brooke being there—without him. The need to protect her was too strong. He couldn't just leave it.

He'd just called his father and informed him that he would not be screening the last two scenes and the show was finished. All he wanted to do now was go and see Brooke and tell her how he felt—even though he knew she probably hated him. Even though he knew she wouldn't want anything to do with him. He wanted to be there after she'd faced that dirt-bag of an ex of hers.

The buzzer went again. The taxi driver was impatient and so was he. With a click of the door, Jack left. He took the stairs two at a time. His stomach was still lodged in his throat, but it dropped quickly when he saw who was at the door.

Brooke.

Standing next to four tall blondes. Somehow, even among that bevy of beautiful Amazonian women, Brooke stood out. To him she always did. Her eyes. Her dimples. Her body. It all made sense to him. It was as if someone had reached into the depths of his mind and pulled out everything he'd ever wanted in a woman and now she was here.

She looked calm. His heart leapt into his throat. Brooke didn't do calm. Something was really up.

The tall blonde standing next to Brooke spoke up. 'Are you Jack Douglas?'

He turned to her and nodded. He didn't want to talk to her—he wanted to talk to Brooke. He wanted to calm her down. Had she seen her ex yet?

'Then I have something to say to you.'

'Maddy, wait…'

Jack turned eagerly towards Brooke's voice. It was quiet and soft and so unlike her that he wanted to step forward and take her in his arms. He wanted her to be his. But he had no idea what she was feeling. Calm Brooke was not someone he'd experienced.

He gripped the strap of his bag hard. 'Brooke. Are you all right?'

'No, she's *not* all right. How could she be all right after what you did?'

'Melissa, stop.'

There it was. Tough Brooke. *His* Brooke.

'I can handle this. Go and wait in the car.'

'We're not leaving you.'

'Go.'

Her voice had become louder. He saw her spark again. His body went tense in anticipation. She was going to tell him off. He hadn't realised till now how much he missed that.

The tall blondes each threw him a look of disdain but they stalked off one by one—the last one putting her fingers to her eyes and then pointing to his before finally leaving him alone with Brooke.

'Jack. We need to talk. Not because I want you back. Don't think that's what I'm here for.'

Jack's heart sank and he had to suck in a few deep breaths. She didn't want him. Now he knew.

'I'm here to ask why? Why you did it?'

'Why I did what?'

She made a sniffing noise and looked away, folding her arms across her chest. When she looked back there were tears in her eyes. She was sad. Angry he could do—but not sad.

Jack stepped forward.

Brooke stepped back. She tried to harden her heart, to keep her emotions in check. It had been easier with her sisters standing beside her, but here alone with him she felt herself waver.

'No. Don't touch me. Don't think you can touch me and make this OK. I want to know why you used what I said against me. Why you lied to me. Why you made me feel like we had something and then threw it all away. For ratings? Or was it for fun? Why would you *do* that? Why would you make me feel like that?'

'Brooke, I did the wrong thing. I thought I was protecting you. I thought that by staying in the background and preventing my father from doing even worse things I was helping you.'

'How did they find out about Mitch? Did *you* tell them?'

This was the question she wanted to know the answer to the most. Had he used the information she'd given to him when she was upset against her? She wanted to hear him say no. She wanted to believe he was good deep down inside.

'Yes, I did.'

Brooke's heart shattered and she stumbled, her act of bravery forgotten for a few seconds.

'But if I hadn't they would have found out some other way. It was going to be worse, Brooke—a lot worse. My father came up with a scheme to trick you all into revealing your feelings about your exes before having them appear. You have no idea how much I fought him on that.'

'You should have fought harder.'

She understood now that he had been trying to help her, but it wasn't enough. He'd let her fall.

'I know I should have. But I realised that too late.'

The tears that threatened Brooke's eyes leapt to the surface. She'd wanted him to fix this. She'd wanted him to be the one. But he wasn't.

'I realise now I'm on my own, Jack. There's no prince coming to rescue me. There's no perfect match for me. I'm going to have to save myself.'

'We all have to save ourselves, Brooke.'

The first teardrop fell. That wasn't what she'd wanted to hear. As much as she knew that she was in this on her own, and that there wasn't a perfect match out there for her, she hadn't wanted it to be true. But it was.

'But that doesn't mean you have to do it on your own.'

Sobs threatened Brooke's chest. She didn't want to listen to him any more. She just wanted to be back with her sisters and hear their comforting words.

'Sometimes you have to be taken out of your comfort zone and be thrown into a completely new situation to see if you sink or swim. And you, Brooke—you're a swimmer. You fought the whole way. For yourself, for the other girls—for women everywhere. There's no doubt in anyone's mind that you are the bravest, toughest woman in Australia right now.'

She *was* brave—he was right. She was tough. But she was still sad that she was alone.

'But no one will ever know how tough you are because I'm not letting the last two episodes go to air. I've cancelled the show. It's over. Everything beyond the football match will never be seen.'

'What?'

Brooke stared at him. What was he saying?

'I told my father to stick it. He can sue me, but those episodes will never see the light of day.'

Brooke's heart leaped. That rollercoaster rocked into view. 'You did that? For me?'

'Of course. I'd do anything for you, Brooke. Because—well, quite frankly, I'd be too frightened of what you'd do to me if I didn't.'

His smile was shy and quiet and genuine. She felt his arms around her, his lips landing on her forehead, her eyelids and her mouth.

'And because...'

Jack stepped forward, but Brooke stepped back again, into the gutter on the street. She was now even tinier. He moved swiftly and grabbed her arms. He wasn't letting her go—not until he'd told her how he felt. She had to know. Everything he'd done was because of her. Because he wanted to protect her. And maybe he was an idiot, and maybe he'd gone about it the wrong way, like he had with his mother, but he wasn't making the mistake of not letting her know how he felt. Not this time.

'I love you.'

Brooke didn't want to cry but she couldn't stop. She was confused and frightened and angry. And Jack was here, telling her what she wanted to hear, and it seemed too good to be true.

'Brooke—listen to me.'

His hands were hot on her arms. He was so close she could smell his scent and it was making her weak. She wanted to fall against him, have him tell her everything was OK, but she wasn't sure. Was this real? Was he telling her that he actually loved her?

'You don't love me, Jack. If you did you wouldn't have let me go so easily.'

Brooke gasped when she felt Jack's arms around her. He lifted her up until her face was level with his.

'Let me tell you something, Brooke. You have no idea how hard it's been for me to let you go. I thought that was what you wanted. I thought you hated me—that you were too angry with me to ever want to be with me again. I thought you didn't want me.'

'I *did* want you.'

She was looking into his eyes now and she saw something. Hurt. Pain. Loneliness. And she knew that was what he could see in hers.

'Do you still want me?'

He was unsure. Big, bold confident Jack was unsure. Brooke's broken little heart started to beat again. Maybe he was telling the truth. Maybe he did love her.

'Yes.' The word came out as a whisper. 'Yes. I still want you.'

The kiss landed on her lips with a force she hadn't been expecting, but he held her steady. Strong and steady. He wanted her. It wasn't over. He hadn't betrayed her. Brooke kissed him back. Hard and furious. She was angry he'd let it come to this and she needed him to know. His kisses trailed down her neck.

'I know you're angry, Brooke. I can feel it.' His lips moved back up to hers. 'And I hope to spend my life making you angry so we can constantly enjoy making up.'

Brooke punched his arm with her fist. Then she kissed him again. Hard.

'Then you need to know one thing, Jack Douglas.' Brooke drank in his smile, his eyes, and the feel of his arms wrapped around her. '*I'm* calling the shots around here.'

* * * * *

Mills & Boon® Hardback
January 2015

ROMANCE

The Secret His Mistress Carried	Lynne Graham
Nine Months to Redeem Him	Jennie Lucas
Fonseca's Fury	Abby Green
The Russian's Ultimatum	Michelle Smart
To Sin with the Tycoon	Cathy Williams
The Last Heir of Monterrato	Andie Brock
Inherited by Her Enemy	Sara Craven
Sheikh's Desert Duty	Maisey Yates
The Honeymoon Arrangement	Joss Wood
Who's Calling the Shots?	Jennifer Rae
The Scandal Behind the Wedding	Bella Frances
The Bridegroom Wishlist	Tanya Wright
Taming the French Tycoon	Rebecca Winters
His Very Convenient Bride	Sophie Pembroke
The Heir's Unexpected Return	Jackie Braun
The Prince She Never Forgot	Scarlet Wilson
A Child to Bind Them	Lucy Clark
The Baby That Changed Her Life	Louisa Heaton

MEDICAL

How to Find a Man in Five Dates	Tina Beckett
Breaking Her No-Dating Rule	Amalie Berlin
It Happened One Night Shift	Amy Andrews
Tamed by Her Army Doc's Touch	Lucy Ryder

Mills & Boon® Large Print
January 2015

ROMANCE

The Housekeeper's Awakening	Sharon Kendrick
More Precious than a Crown	Carol Marinelli
Captured by the Sheikh	Kate Hewitt
A Night in the Prince's Bed	Chantelle Shaw
Damaso Claims His Heir	Annie West
Changing Constantinou's Game	Jennifer Hayward
The Ultimate Revenge	Victoria Parker
Interview with a Tycoon	Cara Colter
Her Boss by Arrangement	Teresa Carpenter
In Her Rival's Arms	Alison Roberts
Frozen Heart, Melting Kiss	Ellie Darkins

HISTORICAL

Lord Havelock's List	Annie Burrows
The Gentleman Rogue	Margaret McPhee
Never Trust a Rebel	Sarah Mallory
Saved by the Viking Warrior	Michelle Styles
The Pirate Hunter	Laura Martin

MEDICAL

200 Harley Street: The Shameless Maverick	Louisa George
200 Harley Street: The Tortured Hero	Amy Andrews
A Home for the Hot-Shot Doc	Dianne Drake
A Doctor's Confession	Dianne Drake
The Accidental Daddy	Meredith Webber
Pregnant with the Soldier's Son	Amy Ruttan

MILLS & BOON®
Hardback – February 2015

ROMANCE

The Redemption of Darius Sterne	Carole Mortimer
The Sultan's Harem Bride	Annie West
Playing by the Greek's Rules	Sarah Morgan
Innocent in His Diamonds	Maya Blake
To Wear His Ring Again	Chantelle Shaw
The Man to Be Reckoned With	Tara Pammi
Claimed by the Sheikh	Rachael Thomas
Delucca's Marriage Contract	Abby Green
Her Brooding Italian Boss	Susan Meier
The Heiress's Secret Baby	Jessica Gilmore
A Pregnancy, a Party & a Proposal	Teresa Carpenter
Best Friend to Wife and Mother?	Caroline Anderson
The Sheikh Doctor's Bride	Meredith Webber
A Baby to Heal Their Hearts	Kate Hardy
One Hot Desert Night	Kristi Gold
Snowed In with Her Ex	Andrea Laurence
Cowgirls Don't Cry	Silver James
Terms of a Texas Marriage	Lauren Canan

MEDICAL

A Date with Her Valentine Doc	Melanie Milburne
It Happened in Paris...	Robin Gianna
Temptation in Paradise	Joanna Neil
The Surgeon's Baby Secret	Amber McKenzie

MILLS & BOON®
Large Print – February 2015

ROMANCE

An Heiress for His Empire — Lucy Monroe
His for a Price — Caitlin Crews
Commanded by the Sheikh — Kate Hewitt
The Valquez Bride — Melanie Milburne
The Uncompromising Italian — Cathy Williams
Prince Hafiz's Only Vice — Susanna Carr
A Deal Before the Altar — Rachael Thomas
The Billionaire in Disguise — Soraya Lane
The Unexpected Honeymoon — Barbara Wallace
A Princess by Christmas — Jennifer Faye
His Reluctant Cinderella — Jessica Gilmore

HISTORICAL

Zachary Black: Duke of Debauchery — Carole Mortimer
The Truth About Lady Felkirk — Christine Merrill
The Courtesan's Book of Secrets — Georgie Lee
Betrayed by His Kiss — Amanda McCabe
Falling for Her Captor — Elisabeth Hobbes

MEDICAL

Tempted by Her Boss — Scarlet Wilson
His Girl From Nowhere — Tina Beckett
Falling For Dr Dimitriou — Anne Fraser
Return of Dr Irresistible — Amalie Berlin
Daring to Date Her Boss — Joanna Neil
A Doctor to Heal Her Heart — Annie Claydon

MILLS & BOON®

Why shop at millsandboon.co.uk?

Each year, thousands of romance readers find their perfect read at millsandboon.co.uk. That's because we're passionate about bringing you the very best romantic fiction. Here are some of the advantages of shopping at www.millsandboon.co.uk:

* **Get new books first**—you'll be able to buy your favourite books one month before they hit the shops

* **Get exclusive discounts**—you'll also be able to buy our specially created monthly collections, with up to 50% off the RRP

* **Find your favourite authors**—latest news, interviews and new releases for all your favourite authors and series on our website, plus ideas for what to try next

* **Join in**—once you've bought your favourite books, don't forget to register with us to rate, review and join in the discussions

Visit **www.millsandboon.co.uk**
for all this and more today!